C000076736

G

TABLE OF CONTENTS

ISSN: 2514-815X △ ISBN: 978-1-8381891-4-3

THE FETCH
ILLUSTRATION
BY ANDREW ROBINSON

EDITOR
Rebecca Parfitt

ASSISTANT EDITOR
Rhys Owain Williams

GRAPHIC DESIGNER
Wallace McBride

ASSISTANT EDITOR
April-Jane Rowan

THE GHASTLING would like to thank J&C Parfitt, Andrew Robinson, Zuzanna Kwiecien, Claire L. Smith and April-Jane Rowan

CONTACT THE GHASTLING

editor@theghastling.com

www.theghastling.com

Social Media: @TheGhastling

PUBLISHED BY THE GHASTLING

Copyright remains with the individual authors and artists. No part of this magazine may be reproduced, except for the purposes of review, without the prior permission of the publisher.

The Ghastling gratefully acknowledges the financial support of the Books Council of Wales.

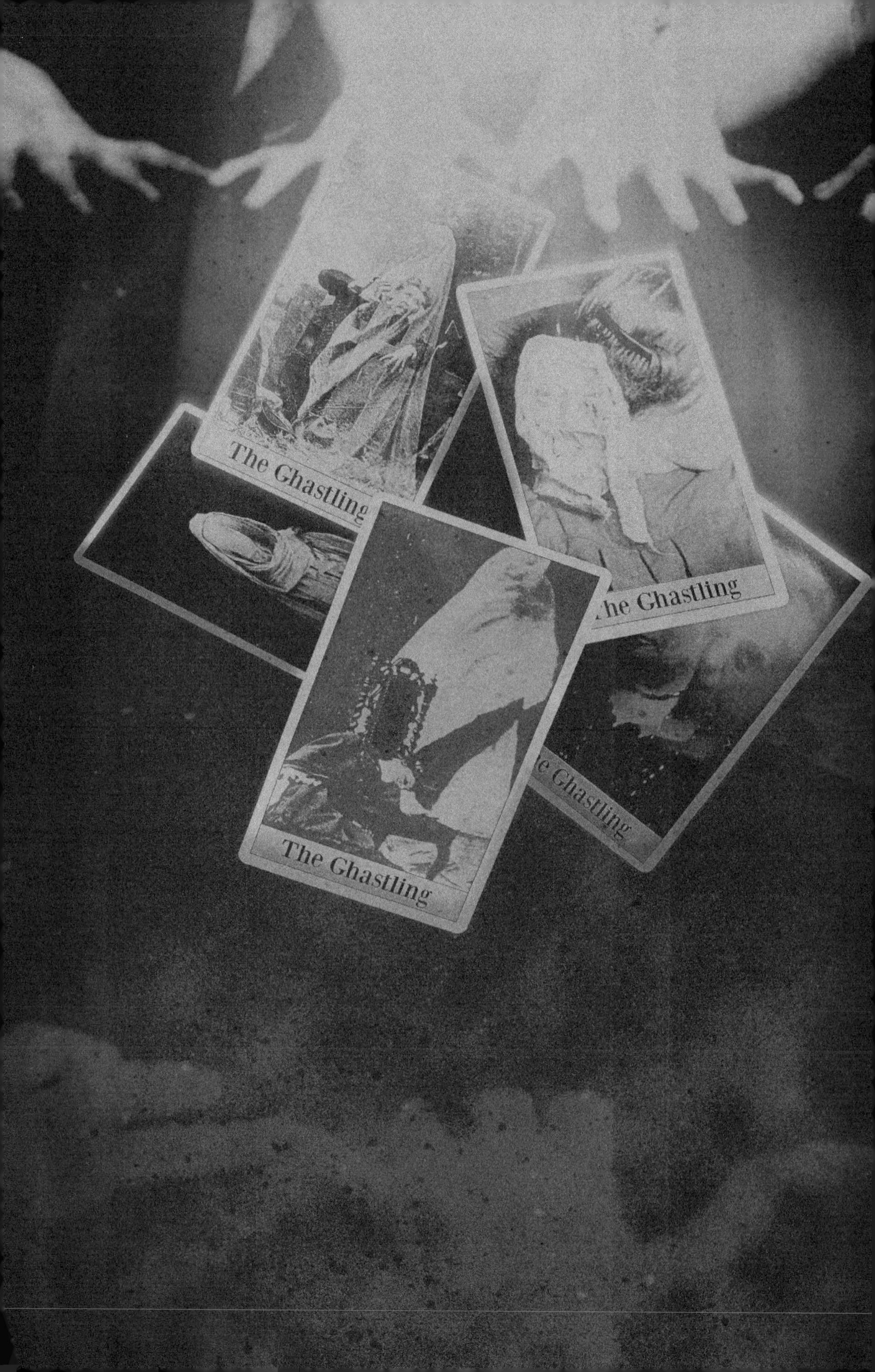
The Ghastling
The Ghastling
The Ghastling
The Ghastling

Patrons of
THE HEADLESS
HORSEMAN

THE FETCH *would like to thank Patreon supporters* AARON SPINK *and*
STEPHEN WHITELAW-KIRK *for sponsoring his omen and keeping impending death alive ...*

VICTORIA DAY
WHO SHOT O'DONOVAN
ROSSA IN DUBLIN

**SANDY DARLENE
LEADINGHAM**
AT LARGE AND
PRESUMED DANGEROUS

MARTHA
NOTORIOUS FOR
THE CORRECT REASONS

FAYE ROBINSON
ACQUITTED BY
A JURY

**CHRISTINE PAMELA
WILLIAMS**
H~~REDACTED~~

LEND US YOUR FEAR
Join The Ghastling on Patreon!

$1

THE ECTOPLASM
You receive our eternal
thanks and access to patron
only feed.

$2

THE SÉANCE
For those who wish to
summon the words: a
monthly writing prompt
straight into your inbox.

$3

THE POLTERGEIST
Your name listed on our
supporter page on the
website, a monthly writing
prompt and access to patron
only feed.

TO JOIN THE PATRONS OF THIS CLUB VISIT PATREON.COM/THEGHASTLING

EDITORIAL

RHYS OWAIN WILLIAMS

Finding strangeness in the familiar is a horror trope that's as old as the genre itself, so it's always a joy to find writers who can tread this motif's well-worn boards and still offer up something that feels fresh and exciting. The eight writers featured in this issue of The Ghastling have done exactly that, uncovering the macabre in the familiar territories of home, work, family and community. And, as some of these stories show, even the very intimate space of our own body can betray us.

In Steven Sheil's domestic horror, expectant father Carl decides to decorate THE PLAYROOM, choosing the colour as a peace offering to his pregnant wife. But opening the old paint tin they'd found in the basement releases more than just fumes, and soon Carl is transported to a strange mirror image of his home, filled with the noises of cavorting animals, squawking birds and the cries of his unborn child.

In HOUSEHOLD, Laura Lee Lucas' child narrator watches the comings and goings of the red house across the street. When the red house's owner Miss Estelle passes away on Halloween night, Daddy says the ambulance men have taken her away. So why, then, is Miss Estelle standing under the big oak tree in her pink bathrobe and slippers? And who else, over the course of this chilling flash fiction, will join her?

Pamela Koehne-Drube's body horror THE ANATOMICAL VENUS gives us a history lesson in 18th-century anatomical models through the eyes of lonely museum curator Dr. Keane, whose only companion in life seems to be the centrepiece of the museum's collection: an alluring cadaver in pearls, sculpted in wax two centuries prior. That is until the arrival of Dr. Evans, whose intentions of business soon give way to pleasure. But there's something about this fellow curator that seems incredibly familiar...

People with common sense don't drive at night through the Berry-Sologne, but with an unwell grandmother somewhere within its tall dark trees, that's exactly what the narrator must do in Astrid Vallet's superb stream-of-consciousness tale LA MAL-BÊTE. As dense fog whirls around both the road and the narrator's mind, the belling of the deer is replaced by more sinister noises in the underwood. The only solution is to keep driving...

Barry Charman's COUNT POLLEN is a folk horror told in interview scraps – as if the Blair Witch had a cousin based in the idyllic English countryside. The eponymous figure of the Count is at the centre of an urban legend steeped in warning, but that isn't enough to stop our inquisitive narrator pursuing the story to the field where black flowers curl like little hands.

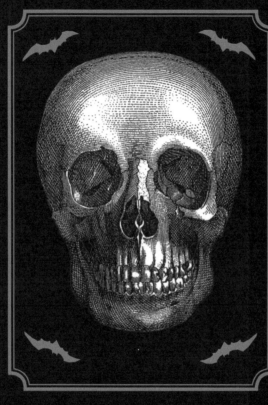

Winona has returned home to help her mother and sisters through A DEATH IN THE FAMILY, but the expected death of her ill father never arrives in Maud Woolf's tale of dark reflections. Instead, Winona finds herself trapped in her childhood home – a house where things aren't quite as she remembers, but still her father locks the door to keep them safe, just like when they were children.

Change is the reason why Marla visits THE OLD MAN in the woods – life had been much simpler before the cramps, the blood and the swelling in

unwanted places. Marla hears from her classmates that the old man can remove what is unwanted, but unfortunately she wants him to take too much in Elin Olausson's disquieting parable of the danger and despair that surrounds body dysmorphia.

And finally, COMING OR GOING by David Towsey takes us to a dystopia of the near future: a landscape familiar in its fish and chips, train stations and children's playgrounds, but where oddness and insecurity reign. And what was that flash of grubby white across the tracks? Why is it that something so quotidian – so everyday – is so feared?

Each of these eight tales offers a descent from the familiar into places alien and uncanny. After reading them, you might begin to see a strangeness in the familiar yourself: an unexpected shape in the corner of your eye, maybe, or an odd noise in the night that you can't quite place. We take no responsibility for you becoming more attuned to these things. Perhaps you will find comfort, though, when we assure you that they have always been there, in the periphery, waiting to be seen.

RHYS OWAIN WILLIAMS
ASSISTANT EDITOR

confusione misit ipius misio...

...tionem qua terram creavit, et per sa...
qua deus diem et mortem ordinavit, et per Ar...
et Archangelos et Tronos dominaciones pri...
et potestates virtutes cherubim et seraphin
per eorum officia, et eorum coniuvationem et per...
per sunt alios, et per eos qui sub ipsius positi sunt, et...
qui deus creavit ad laudem et honorem nominis suo...
...tis, et per firmamentum celi, et per oia ea qui sub fir...
...et per eos relabiles... existit...

THE PLAYROOM

STEVEN SHEIL

The playroom sat at the back of the house, on the opposite side of the hallway to the main bedroom, its single tall window looking down onto the carefully-maintained garden which sat below, and beyond it, the void. Carl stood in the centre of the room and looked at the bare walls which surrounded him.

He'd spent the past day scrubbing them, filling the holes and cracks, sanding down the rough parts and taping up the skirting boards ready for the paint, but now the time had come he felt a pronounced lack of enthusiasm for the task ahead, as though all the energy had been bled from him.

Last evening's argument with Ruth had discomforted him more than he'd acknowledged, he realised now. He'd planned the decoration of the room as a surprise for her, something she would only discover on her return from her parents' house. But she'd seen a payment on the joint account, the money he'd spent this weekend at the DIY shop, and he was too slow to think up a convincing lie.

You're decorating the playroom?
Yes.
Without me?

I thought it would save you the trouble.
Trouble? Trouble...?

At that, the phone had gone dead, almost as though she'd hung up. He'd called back but the line was engaged and when he texted her later that evening, it took her until nearly midnight to respond.

You just have to be in control, don't you?

He hadn't known what to say to that. It wasn't about control so much as about taking care of his responsibilities as a father. He'd thought she'd be happy. At seven-months pregnant she should be thanking him for taking the job off her hands.

The room faced the sun from early morning and was already beginning to get hot and stuffy. Carl put down the cup of tea he'd brought up with him – too warm for hot drinks – went over to the sash window and tried to lift it open. It refused to budge. Painted shut from the outside, he guessed, by whichever idiots had owned the house before. He tried again, straining his arms against the top bar of the frame, but there wasn't even a hint of movement. He gave up and rested his forehead against the cold glass.

He could see something moving in the

branches of the tree that stood between the end of their garden and the void. A squirrel maybe, or one of the pigeons that sometimes sat on his chimney, and whose coos had echoed nightly down into the living-room fireplace until Carl had paid a local firm to place netting over the stacks. Whatever it was, it now left the branches with an almighty leap, sending the whole tree shaking and swaying.

The void was a breeding ground for all sorts of creatures, he'd surmised. Formerly a railway cutting, the void stretched for about a quarter of a mile parallel to the street on which their house sat. He'd been out to look at it when they'd first moved in two years ago, climbing over the rusted iron fence at the end of the garden to inspect the situation. The slope started at only six feet or so from the fence itself, before plummeting near-vertically down a hundred feet or so. The sides and base of the void were thick with greenery – brambles running wild, trees growing askew, branches distending out horizontally into the air like grasping hands. It was nature unkempt, unmanaged, undisturbed and it gave him a sick feeling in his stomach to see it, instilling in him a fear that somehow all that he had could one day be subsumed within it.

He'd built a stronger, taller fence soon after, not so much in the hope that it would keep anything out, but as though to symbolise to the void that a line had been drawn. This garden, this house was his.

He walked back to the centre of the room and knelt by the can of paint that he'd brought up from the basement. This was his concession, his way to tell her that yes, he'd taken her wishes into account. When they'd first moved into the house, before Ruth was even pregnant, they'd stood in this same room and spoken of their plans. There was a certain colour, a kind of brownish red, almost edging to purple, that they'd found on a wall in the basement, painted in the shape of a door (though there was no door there), as though to test it. Ruth had fallen in love with the colour, had wanted it for their bedroom, but Carl had thought a lighter blue – something more calming and tranquil – would suit the space better, and had won out in the end. Now was his chance to offer her something in return.

Looking in the basement for some old curtains to use as dust sheets, Carl had come across a large tin of unlabelled paint. The tin itself looked ancient – rust was eating into the metal on all sides and Carl had feared at first that the whole thing might dissolve in his grip. On the top, carved into the metal in a cursive script which reminded him of the handwriting of a child, was the colour contained within – 'Wild Rose' – and on shaking the tin, there appeared to still be the sound of liquid moving. Placing the tin carefully on the basement floor, Carl had used the tip of a screwdriver to prise open the lid and, as it lifted to show the contents, a waft of strong, sickly scent had hit him, penetrating deep into his nostrils. He had coughed, almost gagged, so forceful had been the smell, but its presence alerted him to the fact that the paint itself was indeed still liquid, still usable. He'd taken the screwdriver and dipped it into the can, stirring the paint itself before bringing it up to the light. There it was, the same red-brown that adorned the basement wall. Ruth's colour.

To tell the truth, it wasn't really right for the playroom, not the way he'd envisaged it anyway. But one wall – the one opposite the window at the back – softened by other colours on the other walls and ceiling would be a good compromise. A statement wall he'd call it when Ruth returned. The statement being *I listened*.

He poured some of the paint into a tray, pressed his roller into it and moved it back and forth, getting a good covering. Then he stood up, approached the wall and placed the roller dead centre, pressing it up towards the ceiling and then dragging it back down to create a thick stripe of colour. He stepped back, looked at what he'd done. The colour seemed different somehow, now that it was up on the wall – deeper, more full-bodied – and for a second or two he wondered if he was making a mistake. Then he moved to one side and the light from the window caught the wall and the colour shifted again to look warm and inviting. The idle thought came to him that when complete it would give the feeling of the womb. He loaded the roller with more paint and went back to work.

By lunchtime he'd completed the first coat and was sweating hard. With no ventilation, the room had become almost unbearably hot and the fumes from the paint combined with the lack of movement in the air had created a stultifying, almost soporific atmosphere. Carl stepped back from the wall and went to rest against the window frame – cursing again the idiot who had rendered it useless – took off his t-shirt and used it to wipe his face and neck, then mopped up the sweat that had

pooled around his sternum.

He stared back across at the painted wall with satisfaction. Wild Rose covered the surface from skirting board to ceiling, and again the richness and fullness of the colour struck him. Seen as a solid block there was a depth to it which was remarkable. It was almost like an optical illusion – the longer you stared at it, the more the wall itself seemed to dissolve away, losing its solidity and becoming something amorphous.

From a long way away Carl seemed to hear animal sounds – the manic squawking of birds, the howl of something dog-like – the whole thing building to an intensity until a loud *thud* at his back sent him leaping away from the window.

Something had hit the glass. He could see a greasy smear in the centre of the window, about the size of a forearm. It had been something big, perhaps a large bird like one of the pigeons. Carl could feel his heart pounding and took a couple of deep breaths to calm himself, in the process inhaling more of the pungent, oily

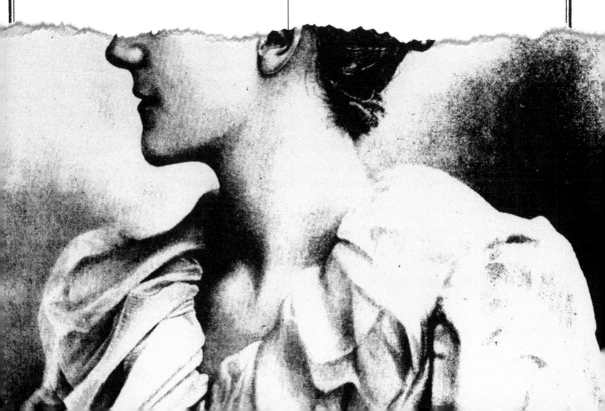

paint smell. He stepped back towards the window and looked down into the garden, half-expecting to see the broken-necked body of a bird lying on the grass beneath. But there was nothing, no sign of any creature, broken or not. Just the smear of its impact distorting the view in front of him.

He cursed again the presence of the void and went back to work. He left his t-shirt off this time, shoving it into the waistband of his cargo pants to use as sweat-rag when needed, and crouched to load the roller once again. The paint gave a *schlucking* sound as he moved it back and forth, and when it was ready he approached the wall and began to apply the second coat.

He started at the top corner nearest the door, with the plan to work methodically along the width of the wall so as to be sure that he was covering every inch. The paint went on even easier with this coat, and he fell quickly into a rhythm which took him from his tiptoes near the ceiling down to a crouch at the floor, before taking a step to the side and beginning again. The light in the room had changed again as the sun had moved around the house and now it was darker than it had been, which gave the paint a browner hue, almost like dried blood. Carl found himself again drawn into the fullness of the paint, its rich and seductive colour. Working now close to the centre of the wall, the colour filled his vision, blotting out any other detail of the room.

Carl could no longer feel his arm moving up and down along the surface, though he could hear the soft, sticky squelch of the paint as it stuck. Beyond that sound came others now, a woman's voice calling out – he couldn't make out what – and the fearful cry of a child. Carl felt himself growing warmer, the air around him thickening. He felt as though he were enclosed, cocooned, held in stasis by some paralysing force. The voices came again – louder, though still indistinct, as though he were hearing them from a distance. He tried

to speak, to answer, but his throat was parched dry as bone and all that emerged was a helpless croak. He felt a sense of terror, an overwhelming sensation of being restrained. Close to panic, he mustered all his energy, forced out a single, rasping *NO!* and twisted away from the wall to fall to his knees.

As he did so he closed his eyes, forcing the colour from his vision. On all fours he found his hands grabbing blindly for the container in front of him, the cold tea from that morning. He lifted it to his lips and drank deeply, letting the liquid fill his dry throat. But even as it passed his lips he knew that there was something wrong. The liquid was thick and glutinous, coating his teeth and tongue, causing him to gag and retch. He opened his eyes, saw that he held not the mug, but the paint pot, a hanging thread of red-brown saliva stretching from its edge to his lips.

He lurched to his feet and scrambled out of the room, running to the bathroom. He turned on the tap and placed his open mouth beneath it, using his fingers to try and scrape the cloying substance from his tongue. His stomach heaved as tendrils of paint snaked down his throat and he coughed hard, spattering the porcelain of the sink with Wild Rose. When finally he'd washed his mouth clean – though still feeling the paint staining his teeth – he sank to his backside on the floor.

Already his mind was rationalising what had happened. The fumes from decades-old paint – who knows what they put in it back then – combined with a lack of ventilation and the heat of the day had driven him delusional, so delusional that he'd mistaken a large tin of paint – different in size, weight and texture – for a mug. He almost laughed to think of it, and if it weren't for the shame involved in losing control in such a way, he might even have considered telling the story next time he and Ruth had friends round. It had been a stupid mistake, nothing more. In his desire to prove to Ruth that he had not been disregarding her wishes, he'd been too cavalier. He should have taken more breaks, or at least made more effort with the window.

He got to his feet and found that his legs were shaking. He leaned on the sink and moved from foot to foot, hoping to reawaken the muscles. As he did so, he glanced into the mirror above the sink. The red-brown paint smeared his face and neck, thick globs hanging in the edges of his neatly-trimmed hair. His lips were heavy with the colour, giving them the appearance of being bruised. Paint stained his chin and marked his bare chest. He looked down at his hands on the sink's edge and saw it wedged deep beneath his fingernails. He had the thought that Ruth wouldn't recognise him if she saw him.

'Get a grip on yourself,' he said to the mirror. But hearing his voice out loud, seeing it come out of the smeared, discoloured lips of his reflection only loosened his sense of certainty, rather than strengthening it. He turned away, closed his eyes and took another deep breath, again tasting the acrid flavour of the paint at the back of his throat. *Get it finished and get out of there,* he told himself, *That's all you have to do.* He opened his eyes and walked out of the bathroom.

He walked into the playroom intending only to put the lid on the paint tin, but on entering the space and seeing his smeared footprints on the bare floorboards leading from the door to the wall, he suddenly felt the same pull that he'd felt before, but even more forceful now, more compelling. In an instant the colour was filling his vision, pulsing almost as though alive. He found himself stepping into the room, stepping ever closer to it, drawn to it by an urge that had been activated deep within him. As he did so, he could hear the sounds again – the animal noises, the woman calling, the baby crying out – each of them getting louder and more insistent.

He was at the wall now, his feet against the skirting board. He felt his arms stretch out as though tugged by invisible strings, and flatten themselves against the surface. At the same time he leant his face and chest against the wall, felt its warmth against his bare skin. The colour was all that he saw now and all that he knew. It surrounded him, enveloped him, pulled him deep within its presence. He felt his body begin to dissolve away at the points where it met the wall, his skin, his muscles, his bones, his blood, all disintegrating painlessly as it engulfed him. And then he was fully within. Formless, incorporeal, suspended in the colour like a specimen in formaldehyde. The noises were all around him now, sounds of animals cavorting. Roars and yelps, growls and hisses. He was somewhere wild, untamed. And again, in amongst the animal sounds, came the cry of a baby.

This time though, there was something different about the cry. Something in the very timbre of the sound resonated through to the very core of him. He knew, somehow, that the voice he was hearing was the voice of his own, yet unborn, child. A child calling out for him, in danger. With a primal fear rising within him, he moved – still formless – towards the sound. As he did so, the colour that surrounded him grew gradually more opaque, until he was looking through it, to a picture that was forming beyond.

He found himself looking out at the playroom again. But the playroom was not as he had left it, raw and unfinished. Instead, it was as though he had somehow moved forward in time to see the room as it would be, a vision from his future. Instead of bare floorboards, the room was filled now with toys and books scattered across a colourful rug. The walls were hung with patterned wallpaper, dotted with cartoon prints of zoo animals. Mobiles hung from the ceiling and moved gently in the air, nudged by the breeze that came from the open window, beyond which lay the dark of night.

As his vision grew clearer, Carl saw a movement at the far end of the room. A shape, squat and low, with elongated, simian arms, withdrawing from the cot which sat in the alcove beside the fireplace, a tightly-wrapped bundle in its grip. The shape scuttled across the rug, pulled itself up to the window ledge, and as it squeezed through, Carl saw the pink face that looked out from the bundle spawn the black hole of a mouth and let out a cry of fear.

A surge of panic went through Carl, a concentration of all his energy and being culminating in a feeling of being wrenched from time and space – and he stepped forward into the room, just in time to see a furry claw letting go of the frame's edge. He was topless still, and paint-smeared, but his body was whole, and his again. He ran to the window and looked out. Down in the garden, lit by the spill from the downstairs window, he saw the creature run across the lawn, something small and pink clutched within its jaws. His baby. His son.

Carl ran from the room and down the stairs. As he turned the corner in the hallway and headed for the kitchen, he thought he heard a voice behind him, a woman crying out – Ruth? – but his mind was too focused on his objective to respond. He burst through the kitchen

and grabbed the handle of the back door, ripping it open and letting it slam against the counter. The creature was at the top of the tall fence now, its large, dog-like body hidden in shadow. Carl saw it glance back at him with orange glinting eyes, before it leapt down into the foliage beyond.

In six long strides, Carl was at the fence. His fingers gripped the top and he planted his foot on the sturdy planks, levering himself up. He swung first one leg, then the other over the top and then was falling into the bushes, landing on his feet amidst a tangle of intertwining branches. He heard the baby cry out again – or perhaps it was another creature – and headed for the sound. Planting his foot in front of him, he felt something give way and in the next moment he was pitched forward into air. As he looked down into the void, Carl thought he could see the darkness at the bottom shift and move, as though with the swarming of beasts, and the thought hit him that he'd come out into a different world, a twisted mirror image of that which he'd left behind, somewhere wilder.

Then he was plunged into the thick greenery which covered the slope and was bouncing, tumbling, over and over, unable to find a handhold to halt his descent, falling helplessly, endlessly, out of control.

"CARNRICK'S"

PEPTONISED (Digested)

COD LIVER OIL AND MILK

Sold by all Chemists in 16 oz. Amber Bottles at 4s. 6d., or sent direct, carriage paid, on receipt of price.

It contains 52 per cent. of pure Norwegian Cod Liver Oil combined with 48 per cent. of evaporated Milk reduced to the consistency of the Oil, both digested. The best, cheapest, and most nourishing emulsion ever made. Sweet as cream. Never separates. The taste of the Oil WHOLLY DISGUISED by the addition of the digested milk. Can be taken by the most delicate person WITH A RELISH. Keeps in any climate. Most emulsions contain 50 to 70 per cent. of water. By using evaporated digested milk instead of water, this preparation is WHOLLY NUTRITIOUS, and therefore the CHEAPEST. A trial of Peptonised Cod Liver Oil and Milk will produce an IMMEDIATE GAIN in FLESH and STRENGTH. Delicate persons and children who have heretofore been unable to take Cod Liver Oil in any form will find the Digested Cod Liver Oil and Milk in this preparation MOST PALATABLE. We also manufacture the above preparation combined with HYPOPHOSPHITES of LIME and SODA.

THE MALTINE MANUFACTURING COMPANY (Limited).

24 and 25, Hart Street, Bloomsbury, London, W.C.

The ONLY GOLD MEDAL at the Health Exhibition for Malt Extracts was given for MALTINE, the only Malt Extract made from Wheat, Oats, and Barley.

Also a GOLD MEDAL for "CARNRICK'S BEEF PEPTONOIDS."

By Special Appointment to
H.M. the QUEEN, H.R.H. the PRINCESS OF WALES,
H.I.M. the EMPRESS OF RUSSIA,
H.M. the QUEEN OF ITALY, H.M. the QUEEN OF the
NETHERLANDS, &c.

REDFERN,
LADIES' TAILOR.

THE
ELECTRICPATENT SOCKS.
FOR CREATING A CONSTANT ELECTRIC CURRENT AND PRODUCING A HIGH DEGREE OF WARMTH.

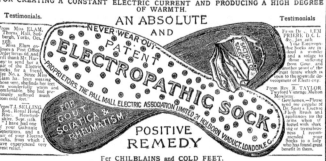

For CHILBLAINS and COLD FEET.

The SOCKS are simply put inside the shoes or boots, and after wearing them a short time a continued and most beneficial warmth penetrates the body.

These ELECTRIC SOCKS prove the best means for keeping the feet warm, for creating bodily comfort, and preventing illness; they are preventive against Rheumatism, Sciatica, and Gout, Chilblains, &c., and also are very beneficial in the first stages of spinal affections, &c. Although the Medical Faculty may disagree upon the true nature of Rheumatic Gout it is beyond doubt that in most cases the most effective remedy is Electricity, which is very effectually conveyed into the system by the use of those Socks worn in boots.

The ELECTRIC SOCKS produce a current acting congenially on the body, and is far superior to the prickling and disagreeable influence of an induction coil. Against spinal complaints, the first symptoms of which are numbness of the feet and pricking sensation (so called "Pins and Needles") they act very effectively, the electric current influencing the spine through the peripheric ends of the nerves.

ELECTRIC SOCKS should be worn by those who have Rheumatic or Gouty Affections in the Feet, or are liable to coldness or chilblains in their parts. The circulation in a torpid state is stimulated, and an agreeable warmth diffused. The heat of the body induces Thermo-Electricity, the generation of this current evolves a galvanic current, and the Electric power is always in force.

IMPORTANCE OF WEARING ELECTRIC SOCKS.—Few are conscious of the very great advantage of wearing under the feet a medium that will not only prevent the abstraction of electricity by cold earth, but will at the same time generate in the feet those electric currents on which health depends.

Please forward Exact size of Feet when ordering these Socks. All Chemists keep the Electricpatent Socks.

VETEEN.

S VELVETEEN has already
the world of fashion than that
and when we take into con-
all occasions—an advantage no
employed as a complete dress,
effective as it is serviceable, its

PLATT & CO., 3/, St. Martin's
Lane, London, W.C. will send free to any part
of England, Ireland, or Scotland, on receipt of cash
with order—

First quality, 1 lb., 3s. 3d.; 2 lbs., 6s. 3d.; 4 lbs., 12s.
and 1s. extra for every further lb.

Second quality, 1 lb., 2s. 9d.; 2 lbs., 5s. 3d.; 4 lbs., 10s.,
and 1s. 6d. extra for every further lb.

Third quality, 1 lb., 2s. 3d.; 2 lbs., 4s. 3d.; 4 lbs., 8s.,
and 2s. extra for every further lb.

N.B.—If 24 lbs. are ordered we charge 1d. per lb.
less; if 32 lbs., 2d. per lb. less.

18-c. HEAVY ROLLED GOLD

27s.

SCARF PIN, GOLD, 15s.
Smaller, 10s. and 12s.
CASE, 1s. 6d.

es of Fairyland Caught by Camer

reature at the left is. posed on bush leaves offering a posey of ha
esh-and-blood friend. The leaping fairy at play with another litt
shown at the right.

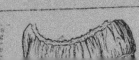

AL IRREGULARITIES
N. I was despairing
ended your Electro-
of it, but I shall be

BRONCHITIS.

The Rev. E. AUBREY, Rose, Cottage, 130,
Ystrad Road, Ystrad, Pontypridd, writes, Jan.
1885:—"I have great pleasure in giving a
favourable report of the Child's Lung In-
... received last October for a little
... from Bron-

before, because I
wish I had purch
thankfully, C HIT

LIVER COM

THE ANATOMICAL VENUS

PAMELA KOEHNE-DRUBE

ILLUSTRATED BY CLAIRE L. SMITH

M ine was a solitary world: a world where life and death intertwined, one indistinguishable from the next. There weren't many visitors to the museum these days as interest in the medical curiosities of a bygone age had waned. People were more concerned with bright and happy things, not in darkness and the inevitability of death.

I made my rounds of the exhibits, trying to ignore the few snatches of conversation that punctuated the silence, echoing off the building's vaulted ceilings. There were two types of people who walked my hallowed halls. Scholars with an academic interest in medical history or teenagers who came to gawk in morbid fascination at the displays. I cared for neither. The academics always wanted to talk, and the teenagers just wanted to point and laugh, so I tended to walk the floor shortly before closing.

It was my favourite time of day – those few visitors we had were mostly gone, and the museum shone with old light. The last remaining rays of the sun glimmered through the heavy, leadlight windows, airborne dust dancing within its cutting beams. The rooms smelled musty, comforting, like old bones, mildew, and rotting cloth. The objects stood sentinel, reminders of an age long past when things were simple and death omnipresent. While wax cracked and the textiles decayed, there was beauty in that decline.

I reached into one of the cases, brushing away the scat that speckled the black velvet base with a gloved hand. *Anthrenus museorum* – museum beetles – were a constant source of terror in my line of work. But I didn't feel the same disgust for them as others in my field. Despite the unfathomable destruction they wreaked on the collections, they were an integral part of the circle of life. Whatever organic matter remained on our specimens, the beetles would chew up and excrete into the very dust that the visitors breathed. There was something poetic in that – a balance of the natural and the unnatural in perfect unity.

In every cabinet along every wall stood examples of the wonder of nature. One room housed a skeleton fused in an intricate display of ossification caused by Stone Man Syndrome. It was lace-like and delicate, beautiful despite the horrific death of the body it once inhabited. Another housed the jarred and preserved bodies of conjoined twins. Born prematurely, they were too weak to live, their tiny bodies merged in a grim simulation of love. I was often moved by their little arms curled around each other as if seeking protection from prying, curious eyes. To many, these were grim reminders of their own mortality, but to me, they proved resilience. While others would die and be forgotten, the specimens in my collection would live on.

I was so lost in thought that I almost walked into a woman who stood silently, examining my favourite exhibit.

'Sorry,' I mumbled, trying to mask my irritation at the fact she'd been in my way.

She waved away my apology and smiled, her cheeks dimpling as she did so. She was familiar somehow, in a way I couldn't place, and her eyes twinkled with intelligence as I stared at her blankly.

I have never had good relationships with people. Even as a child, I found conversation awkward and uncomfortable. People always had expectations, and I never said the right things. I tried to smile back, but I felt myself grimace instead. I opened my mouth to speak but found no sound, my lips flapping uselessly like a fish out of water. I could see the pity behind the woman's eyes at my pathetic attempt at normal human interaction, and I wished the ground would swallow me up so this moment could end.

Thankfully, the woman continued, ending the awkward silence.

'Doctor Allison Keane, I presume?' she said, holding her hand out in greeting.

'Yes,' I managed to stammer out. 'And you are?'

'Doctor Elizabeth Evans, curator at Starmley. I'm a long admirer of your work in the preservation of wax figures,' she indicated downward with a wave of her hand, 'and wanted to talk to you about expanding our collections.'

We were standing over the pride and centrepiece of the museum: The Anatomical Venus.

How many times had I stood here by the Venus' prone form, taking in every detail? I habitually looked for any changes in her that would require my immediate attention, although I admit that I probably paid her more attention than was strictly needed. I lowered my gaze. Looking at her through the eyes of a new observer was like seeing her for the very first time.

The Venus lay on a bed of purple velvet. Her wax skin was milky white, and her pale-brown, real human hair fanned around her face like a halo contrasting starkly with the dark fabric. Her body was twisted at an odd angle, her head turned to the side, eyes hooded, lips slightly parted as if in pleasure. The entire tableau evoked a sense of ecstasy, and it never failed to elicit a visceral longing within me.

She was naked, save for a string of chaste, white pearls at her throat. The elegant curve of her neck widened out to the swell of her breasts, perfectly formed. Sometimes, when the museum was cold and quiet, I could swear I saw them rise and fall as if she breathed. Despite her peaceful visage, she was violently laid open and virtually unadorned, just as nature had made her. Her inner organs coiled like the pearls she wore at her throat in a cavity that went from chest to abdomen. Someone had exposed her for the world to see. Not only had her creator captured the moment of ecstasy, but it lay her most private parts, her inner self bare for the masses.

There weren't many like her left, but I considered her the most beautiful thing I had ever seen. I stayed behind most nights to watch her sleep. That's how I saw her – a sleeping goddess.

I wasn't the first to observe her like this, of course. She was over 200 years old and had been in the company of many men in that time. I wasn't so deluded as to think I was unique in my admiration. Countless male hands had reached inside her, plucking out her organs, one by one, layer by layer, as they studied her. At the time of her creation, cadavers had been hard to come by and she served in their place, letting the men who studied desecrate her as she lay dreaming, perfect, and pristine; seductive despite her visage of death.

We had many other anatomical models at the museum, but none like my Venus. She was perfect – one of a kind.

Sensing where my mind had wandered, Doctor Evans picked up the thread. She lowered her own gaze to the Venus and sighed in appreciation.

'Not many Venus models have survived in such a wonderful state of preservation,' she let her eyes wander over the prostrate body below. 'You've done a wonderful job, and I can see why you're such an authority on them.'

I nodded, pride swelling in my chest at the compliment. This was territory that I knew and understood. This was something I could talk comfortably about. I took great pains to ensure my collections were pristine, and while I didn't seek the admiration of my peers, it was still nice to know I had it. The museum's visitors mostly took it for granted that the objects would be there for their amusement. They didn't care to know or understand the painstaking labour that went into keeping destruction at bay.

'She's a special case. I've tried to keep her as original as possible. I've had to replace parts over the years,' I motioned to the pearls at her throat, 'but I always try to stay true to her essence. With the materials available, though, there's only so much I can do.'

'She looks so real. So lifelike,' the reverence in the Doctor's voice was palpable. 'It's why I came to you. We're accessioning a collection of wax figures, and I wanted your advice on preparation and preservation.'

'I could make you an appointment for tomorrow?'

She shook her head

'No, sorry, I'm only here for a quick visit. I leave first thing in the morning, so I'm afraid we'll have to dispense with formalities. I was hoping we could organise a week's residency for you at Starmley...'

The thought of leaving my Venus almost sent me into a blind panic, and Doctor Evans must have sensed it because she quickly continued.

'Or, if you have no plans for this evening, I could take you to dinner at the university's expense? You could help me draft an initial preservation plan that we can flesh out and communicate on via email?'

Now I was torn between relief and panic. I was relieved at knowing I could stay with my Venus but terrified of an evening of making small talk and play-acting at social niceties. My face went blank, and I froze like a rabbit cornered by a fox, alert and frightened. Business meetings didn't usually run to the social. Business I could work with – I knew what to do in a professional setting. Outside of that, I was always nervous and never knew quite what to say or how to behave, but as I looked at Doctor Evans, the refusal I was about to utter died on my lips. The way she tilted her head quizzically waiting for my answer struck me as oddly familiar, like an old friend whose memory had grown hazy with time.

I pushed my panic down, Doctor Evans' familiarity putting me strangely at ease. Besides, I was a professional and I had a duty of care, not only to my own collections, but to help others care for theirs. My desire to preserve overcame my social awkwardness, and so I agreed. Better an evening of anxiety than a week away from the objects I so loved.

We started our dinner with a few fumbling attempts at small talk, but it wasn't long before we found a rhythm. We had a shared interest and professional courtesy that could sustain our first, awkward moments, and the more time I spent in Doctor Evans' company, the more I felt like I knew her.

After work was out of the way and our meals finished, something started to shift, almost imperceptibly. That nagging familiarity I felt with Doctor Evans was growing. She had a habit of shaking her head when she laughed, making her hair fan around her shoulders in a gentle wave. Whenever she did that, a recognisable smell would waft toward me – a scent I couldn't quite place but that felt as familiar to me as my own skin. I was in uncharted waters, exposed in a way I wasn't used to.

Despite a relatively symmetrical face, a straight nose, and large, bright eyes, I'd never taken too much pride in my appearance. My aesthetically-pleasing face, but lack of vanity, had allowed me a certain measure of invisibility. I preferred it that way – hiding behind unremarkable anonymity. My obsession with work had always made me unapproachable, so relationships had been rare. The subtle change in how the Doctor and I responded to each other was new to me, but it wasn't entirely unpleasant. She appeared to be transforming, or perhaps it was just my perception of her that was changing, but I decided to relax and just enjoy the evening.

With that acceptance, time flew. We shared stories and she spoke about the history of her collections with a passion born of experience. I told her about my study of anatomy, and she told me of her travels to far-flung destinations, collecting rare objects that would otherwise have been lost to time.

I was enthralled by her stories. She painted pictures with her words. She didn't just love her objects, she lived and breathed them, and spoke with so much authority that I could almost have believed she'd experienced their history herself. She spoke of the dead as if they were still with us, fresh in her memory, rather than long gone and relegated to books. I put it down to our roles at our respective museums. She was a curator, and I was a conservator. Where I preserved objects, she told their stories. Where I made them look lifelike, she brought them to life through narrative. I sought to stop decay through science, but her words would ensure that the collections would live forever in the public imagination.

All my life, I'd been an outsider, my fascination with the dead making those around me uncomfortable. Even my own parents, who supported my odd hobbies like collecting and mounting exotic insect specimens, had never truly understood me.

Doctor Evans – *Elizabeth*, I corrected – seemed to understand me perfectly. For the first time, I didn't have to hide that part of myself. I talked to her about my early years creating art from animal bones and my interest in dissection and human anatomy. We spoke about historical medical practises, but when I expressed my admiration for the Venuses and the men who had created them, she seemed to withdraw a little. It was then that the nagging thought I'd had since Elizabeth and I first met finally burst into my mind, fully realised.

She looked and smelled exactly like Venus! She had the same flawless, pale skin, the same hair, the same lips. How many hours had I spent caressing the Venus, disassembling and reassembling her body, imagining her movements, desperate to feel cold wax give way to real flesh? I was fascinated by her, and here was her living twin. How had I not seen it sooner?

When she reached out to grasp my hand, it was as if the universe had revealed a fundamental truth. My Venus had simply been a chrysalis waiting to reach its final form, and that form sat right here, in front of me. As her fingers closed around mine, I looked into her eyes with fascination. She smiled at me, knowingly.

'I wonder who she was?' I was caught off guard by her intuition – there could be no doubt she was talking about my Venus.

'I'd never considered that before,' I said, genuinely surprised by the question. 'I always saw her as a representation of perfection, dreamed up by her creator, Clemente Susini, never as a portrayal of someone real.'

'Susini modelled his figures from real corpses though, so she must have at least been inspired by someone, surely?'

'Maybe, but I don't think that's what makes her so fascinating.'

'Oh?' Elizabeth raised an eyebrow, and I couldn't help but feel this was some kind of test.

'Well,' I cleared my throat nervously, 'she comes from a time when the study of medicine was still in its infancy. Dissections weren't just carried out by medical professionals, but by artists. Even Da Vinci cut up bodies to fuel his artistic expression. She was a way to get people interested. To seduce them into human betterment by making death itself seductive.'

'The seduction of oblivion. Interesting.'

'It fascinates us all – the fear of not knowing what happens after we die. Our bodies decay, and we disappear from the world, but her? She's permanent. Incorruptible. Susini made her that way and I've continued his legacy. She transcends the fear of death and shows that, despite its inevitability, there is still beauty in it.'

'But what about the woman she was? Doesn't her story deserve to be told on her own terms, rather than through the desires of the men who made her?'

'They made her immortal,' I shrugged. 'Preserved at the moment she was most beautiful. Isn't that, ultimately, what we all want?'

She gave my words some consideration, and I thought I'd said something wrong until she leaned across the table, pulling my head forward and kissing me deeply. It was unexpected and I tensed, but as her hair brushed my cheeks I was surrounded by the familiar mildew scent of the museum, finally recognising it for what it was. Its familiarity calmed me. I gave myself over to the kiss, drawing her close and returning it with reckless abandon.

When she pulled back, I smiled crookedly, but she just stared at me with a sharp look.

'Do you want to get out of here?'

'Out of here?' I mimicked, inwardly cursing myself.

At first, I couldn't quite grasp her meaning, but when it finally dawned on me, I felt my cheeks flush with expectation.

'I have a bottle of wine at home', I stammered, my mouth going dry, and my stomach knotting with nerves. 'It's only a short walk.'

She waved over the waiter with a smile and paid our bill as we headed out the door into the darkness beyond. It was the first time anyone had ever bought me dinner. I tried to remind myself that it was always the arrangement, but imagining the evening was even tangentially work-related at this point seemed ludicrous given the current circumstances.

We kissed again in the moonlight on a bridge overlooking the river. The light glanced across the water like sprites taking wing. She drew me in, her lips soft and inviting, and I felt myself responding to her in a way I never had with another person. I gave myself over to her familiar scent. The museum smell was intoxicating, calming me like only the objects in my care ever could. I thought of my

Venus then, imagining she was the one in my arms.

I hardly knew how to navigate the sensations suddenly flooding my body. Change bred uncertainty, but somehow, in this moment, I'd never been more certain of anything in my life. Everything felt natural and right, as if this night had been created just for me, the promise of perfection waiting just around the corner.

I unlocked the heavy wooden doors to my home, ushering her in, giving her a few moments to wander its twisting halls as I left to fetch a bottle of wine from the kitchen.

I'd never lived anywhere but my dark, Victorian terrace. It was where I'd grown up and was left to me after my parents passed. They'd been keen collectors of antiques, and I'd always been proud to maintain their legacy. I treated their belongings like I would any museum exhibit but had added my own unique flourishes over the years.

As I returned from the kitchen, I stopped to watch Elizabeth. I was struck by how much more alive my home seemed with her in it. She moved through the darkened hallways like a ray of light, bringing a warmth to them that they usually lacked. It made me uncomfortable, but I pushed the thought aside. The walls were cluttered floor to ceiling with images and specimens, and she looked around curiously, taking her time, observing my collections with the keen eye of a fellow appreciator.

Butterflies, moths, and beetles, displayed behind glass adorned the walls. I held my breath in anticipation as she stopped at a glass cabinet of taxidermied birds, the pride of my personal collection. I'd meticulously planned and constructed the diorama, carefully posing each hand-picked bird to mimic flight. They appeared to flitter among the branches of the dead tree that displayed them and having an accomplished artist like the doctor show appreciation made my heart swell with pride. The human anatomical drawings I'd collected over the years were of particular interest to her, and I followed her movements as she gently traced her fingers along the sweeping lines of one of the larger pieces with natural grace.

She stopped outside my bedroom, and as I moved to hand her a glass, she took my wrist and led me inside. Yesterday this situation would have made me uncomfortable. But not tonight. Tonight was for new beginnings.

Taking the wine bottle from my trembling hands, she poured us both a glass. She watched me with hooded eyes as I took a shuddering swig to calm my nerves. I barely had time to put the glass down before she pulled me down onto the bed, taking me in her arms. Flipping me onto my back, she leant down to kiss me, and I tasted the sweet, heady flavour of wine against her lips.

'Don't think,' she whispered, and so, I didn't. I gave myself over wholly to her embrace.

There was something wild about the way we made love, animalistic and primal. We'd been careful and cautious, tiptoeing around each other until this moment. Our words had been calculated and well-reasoned like cogs in a well-oiled machine, but our actions now were the opposite. Instead, we ran on instinct, leaving me feeling dirty. What had felt pristine and perfect just a moment ago had flown, leaving something base and filthy in its wake – a mess of fluid and flesh.

I tried to give myself over to my physical nature, but it was becoming impossible to ignore the turmoil of unease building in my mind. The spell of the evening was broken. Tarnished. I continued to go through the motions but closed my eyes and longed for the peace and silence of the museum, thinking instead of the Venus and her sleeping form.

When I finally opened my eyes and looked at Elizabeth, I saw her head tilt and her eyes roll back at the moment of ecstasy. Finally, I saw it.

That spark of recognition I'd felt from the first resolved itself into a realisation so profound that it took my breath away. She *was* my Venus.

I was so lost in that realisation that I barely registered her leaning to retrieve something from her discarded belongings. I felt a sharp pain in my sternum and started, knocking my wine off the bedside cabinet in shock. I blinked at her in confusion before looking down, watching almost dispassionately as she slowly and methodically dragged a shining silver scalpel between my breasts, down to my abdomen.

As realisation finally dawned, my eyes widened in shock and pain. Almost mechanically, I turned my head to watch my blood mingle with the red wine spreading against the white of the sheets. It was beautiful, I thought.

I lay there stunned, paralysed by agony, and yet felt oddly calm as she buried her hands in my flesh. She was my Venus. How many times had I done the same to her? How many times had I reached inside her body to remove her organs for nothing more than my own gratification? With a crack, she laid me open, and I finally screamed. She just sat there, watching my exposed heart as it fluttered weakly.

Through the pain came clarity, and I knew these were the last moments of my life. Tears of hurt and shame stung my eyes. I imagined myself as she must see me – my inner beauty on display for her viewing pleasure. I was prone, laid open, and bare, nothing more than an object for study.

As the darkness of oblivion finally came to take me, the last thing I saw was her reaching over my head to pluck something from the corner of the bedhead. It was where I kept a single strand of pure, white pearls – a secret memento of my Venus. Placing them around my neck, she leaned down and whispered to me.

'Now you are perfect. Immortal. Your beauty will be preserved.'

HOUSEHOLD

LAURA LEE LUCAS

ILLUSTRATED BY ZUZANNA KWIECIEN

No one lives in the red house now. When Miss Estelle lived in the red house, my brother Malik would shovel the snow off her sidewalks and rake the leaves off her lawn for crumpled dollar bills. Miss Estelle would stand under the porch light of the red house at night sometimes and look at our apartment building, or back and forth across the street. She would shield her eyes with one hand like the sun was out, even though it was dark.

On Halloween night Mama took me trick-or-treating. When we came home Daddy and Malik said Miss Estelle was dead. There was a ghost on her front porch, a white sheet with something underneath that was bright from the porch light. The ambulance men pushed it down the walk, into the ambulance with all the lights off. Daddy said it was Miss Estelle.

But he was wrong because Miss Estelle was standing under the big oak tree at the corner. I could see her pink bathrobe and slippers. When I told Malik, he said I should go to bed.

✦✦✦

Then the Iannaccones moved into the red house. They had three sons. Vinnie and Paulie and Dave were tall and blond. They said lots of bad words that Mama didn't like. At school they were always loud, but on the bus home, the closer they got to the red house, the less they spoke. Daddy said their upstairs lights were on all night every night and the porch light too. He told Mama he didn't know how they could sleep.

✦✦✦

The night Malik went to the junior prom, Vinnie Iannaccone was supposed to go too. Malik heard Vinnie brag about his date and the limo he was gonna get, except Vinnie never came. Malik said Vinnie's date was mad because he didn't pick her up and she had to take an Uber to the dance. That night, Vinnie's window stayed dark.

Mrs. Iannaccone left the porch light on. She kept peeking out the curtains, looking for Vinnie. She was still there when I fell asleep.

The next day there were two police cars outside the red house. The lights on top spun round and round.

The police looked for Vinnie for days. They didn't find him.

Mama went over to the red house with a casserole. Mama talked to Mrs. Iannaccone and they sat in chairs on the porch.

It started to get dark. A car went past the red house with its headlights on. When it turned at the corner, the lights lit up the big oak tree. Vinnie was standing under the tree, dressed in a black suit with a pink flower on his chest.

'Mama!' I called out my window. My mama turned her head. 'Look!' I pointed at the oak tree. The car and lights were gone and so was Vinnie.

'Look at what?' Mama said.

The next Sunday the Iannaccones moved out. A 'For Sale' sign was in front of the red house on Tuesday.

This afternoon, Daddy came out of the red house with a man. They shook hands and the man left.

Daddy walked down the front walk. The sun was setting behind the red house. Daddy was whistling and smiling. The porch light came on behind him. Then a light turned on upstairs, in Vinnie's old window. Daddy didn't see them.

Tonight after I went to bed it started to rain. I couldn't sleep for all the tap-tap-ping so I got up and looked out my window. The street was dark and slick and wet and the cars made everything shine funny with their lights.

I didn't want to, but I looked in the shadow under the oak tree.

Miss Estelle and Vinnie Iannaccone were both there, staring up at me. Their hair wasn't wet, or their clothes. Miss Estelle waved her hand like she wanted me to come down, in the rain, in the dark. A light came on in the tiny window at the top of the red house. It was right across from mine.

I shut my curtains fast.

Daddy and Mama are talking in their room, real quiet, but I can hear them through the heat vents in the wall. 'No more renting?' Mama asks. 'It's all ours!' Daddy says happily, and they laugh together.

Behind my curtains I can still see the lights from the windows and the porch that no one turned on and I'm scared, I'm scared, I'm so afraid that someone lives in the red house now.

PATENT LITERARY MACHINE
For holding a book or writing desk, lamp, &c., in any position, over an easy chair, bed, or sofa, obviating the fatigue and inconvenience of incessant stooping while reading or writing. Invaluable to invalids and students. Admirably adapted for India. A most useful gift. Prices from £1 1s. Illustrated Price List Post Free.

TRADE MARK, REGISTERED.

BREAKFAST IN BED.
CARTER'S PATENT RE-VOLVING BED-TABLE. Adjustable to any height or inclination, for reading or writing. Prices from £2 5s. Illustrated Price List Post Free

TRADE MARK REGISTERED.

INVALID FURNITURE
Invalid Adjustable Couches and Beds, from £5 10s. ; Wicker Bath Chairs, £2 2s. ; Exercising Chairs, with Horse Action for Indigestion, £5 5s. ; Carrying Chairs, £2 10s. 6d. ; Reclining Boards, £2 5s. ; Trapped Commodes, £1 5s. ; Perambulators, £2 5s. ; Leg Rests, £1 10s. ; Back Rests, 11s. 6d. ; Self-propelling Chairs, £6 10s. ; Bed Tables, from £1 each, &c. Illustrated Price List Post Free.

BATH CHAIRS
In Wicker, from £2 2s.

INVALID CARRIAGES
of all kinds at low prices.

J. CARTER, 6a, New Cavendish Street, Portland Place, London, W.

WRITING TABLE AND BOOK-CASE, Walnut or Ebonized Drawers and Cupboards at sides, 3 ft. and 3 ft. 6 in., £9 and £9 15s.

PAVEMENT, FINSBURY, LONDON, E.C.
(CLOSE TO MOORGATE STREET RAILWAY STATION.)

Furniture of good design and make at very moderate cost.

EARLY ENGLISH SUITES OF DRAWING ROOM FURNITURE, from 15 Guineas.

DINING ROOM SUITES, from £18 Gs.
BED ROOM SUITES, from 9 Gs.

CATALOGUES FREE.

THE MOST PERFECT AERATED NON-ALCOHOLIC BEVERAGE.

NON-ALCOHOLIC SPARKLING DELICIOUS EXHILARATING GRATEFUL AT HOME

VIN-SANTÉ.
(SWEET OR DRY). Registered.
CONTAINING HYPOPHOSPHITES.

FOR BALLS
FOR PICNICS
FOR DINNERS
FOR SUPPERS
AT CLUBS
AT ALL TIMES

Taken with meals stimulates the Appetite and assists Digestion. Contains in the most assimilable forms those *Hypophosphites* which are so valuable for their *invigorating tonic and restorative* properties combined with iron. Write to any of Agents for Descriptive Pamphlet, which will be sent post free, and which contains a few selected Testimonials from ladies, medical men, and others.
The only Prize Medal given to Aerated Beverages at International Food Exhibition was awarded to Vin-Sante.
Manufactured by the Vin-Sante and Non-Alcoholic Beverage Company, Limited, Liverpool.
Sold Retail, in Champagne quarts, at 10s. 6d. per dozen, Champagne pints, 6s. 6d. dozen, by Grocers, Druggists, Wine Merchants, &c., everywhere. Sole Wholesale Agents—EVANS, SONS, and CO., Liverpool. Special Agents—EVANS, LESCHER, & WEBB, London ; and CROSSE & BLACKWELL, London.

RISH LINENS
AND CAMBRIC HANDKERCHIEFS
JAMES LINDSAY & CO.
(LIMITED),
BLEACHERS, MANUFACTURERS, AND MERCHANTS, BELFAST.
ESTABLISHED OVER FIFTY YEARS.
will forward to any Railway Station, carriage paid on parcels of £5 and upwards in value.

" MONTSERRAT "
Lime-Fruit Juice, Limetta, or Pure Lime-Juice Cordial, also Aromatic, Clove, Jargonelle, Peppermint, Pineapple, Quinine,

LA MALBÊTE

ASTRID VALLET

I grunt and stretch and push the card into the slit, and the light turns green and the barrier lifts before the machine is even done printing out the ticket, and I stretch and grunt and snatch the card and the damn ticket and toss all that onto the passenger seat, and scramble to start the car again. It purrs and moves on and the barrier doesn't slam onto the roof, I wonder if that ever happens. I also tell myself that October is simultaneously the best and worst time for a short trip into the Berry like this, mostly the worst, and then I realise my window is still down. My eyes are still on the road because at this point I don't know where I'm going, I fumble in the dark for the button and the window glides back up. Still the worst time. Well, this road here sorta looks familiar, and it's well lit. Who knew these small dying towns still had the budget for streetlights? I dunno why I flick my blinker on.

Sure, this looks about right, for now. I decide I'm not in the mood to play guessing games for the rest of the way and bring the car into the parking lot of the church. This town seems like it's gonna be the last bit of civilisation for a while, but wouldn't you know it, already I don't have much signal. The GPS app is taking forever to load, I look around,

squinting at the outside. I can feel a bubble of migraine start swelling at the back of my head, partly because of the AC, the freshness of it and the noise it makes. But it's gotta stay on, I can't deal with condensation on the windshield on top of everything else.

The best and worst time. I'm cradling the phone, as though that helps. I couldn't care less about the stag-belling season, I dunno what it is about the stag-belling season that arouses such wonder and nostalgia in Berry people. Just a bunch of horny animals screaming. That's supposed to be the 'best part'. I wanna put the heat on, but something tells me that'll make more condensation. I dunno how anything works. I reach into the back seat for my leather coat and my scarf, and I pull them on. It's my dad's leather coat, actually, it's too big for me, but it makes me feel like a big girl.

The best and worst time. I tuck the phone between my thighs. The directions are all loaded, final-fucking-ly. Why the worst? Because it's October, and night falls early, and people with common sense don't drive at night through the Berry-Sologne. I have common sense, I do, but granma's not well, so I hear, has to do with her having lost her cat. I pass the sign, leaving the town behind. It feels colder without the streetlights standing around in orange light.

I grip the wheel. It's cold, my fingers are cold. I wanna go faster, I'd go faster if the road was smoother. When did I last pump up my tires? That being said, it's looking like the road is gonna be straight for a while. Tentatively, I press a little harder on the gas, and it's not too bad, it's manageable. Tall dark trees speed past, almost to a blur. There are little eyes that catch the lights on either side, high and low, mostly low, low to the ground. Rabbits. No, hares. Hares? Surely that's what they're called. And pheasants. Granma always said only to watch out for the boars.

Patches of fog make me ease off the gas, and I'm very reluctant, because I want a warm meal and a warm bed right now, but I'd rather not end up in a ditch. But it feels nice to take up speed again once the car emerges.

There's more road left than I thought, and the drive's already longer than I remember. Oh to be a kid dozing off in the backseat. I regularly check my phone, still, but the screen stares right back, offended by my doubt, and the direction of the blue arrow doesn't change one bit. There used to be more villages, maybe they really did die, maybe they dissolved, because it's all woods and fields and streetlights standing in the dark now.

There are screams, loud but distant and eerie, deformed by the echo, or lack thereof. I used to be scared of the stags belling, belling and belling. Until that one night when I was shoved into a car for 'a surprise', and brought to the edge of a field, and granma and ma held my hands and showed me the stags, belling and belling. That was a small epiphany for little me. I couldn't decide if it was beautiful or ridiculous, but certainly it wasn't scary. Now I'd say it's overrated, and I find myself wishing they'd just mate and shut up, because it's all lost its magic. This is already too long of a drive.

I try for the radio and it screams white noise and fragments at me. Nevermind.

The thought that granma's dead crosses my mind. I dunno what I'd do. One awful part of me knows I'd be pissed to have come all this way for nothing, all this way through the Berry, at night, with pots and jars shivering in front of the passenger seat, emptied of the jam and kirsch cherries they'd contained, all that to bring them back to a dead granma like some absurd little Red Riding Hood. Last I heard of her she was kneading bread and brioche to welcome me with, and really there's no reason for me to think she's dead, but that's where my mind's going, I think if she knew she'd forgive me.

Another patch of fog swallows the car whole and I sigh, this one's so dense I have to slow down. I jump when a message dings in and I look down, and apparently granma can text now: *Do you have your gri-gri on?* But there's a stone cross and it's running at me and I slam on the brakes and both the car and the cross stop. The motor coughed and stalled and I couldn't care less. I stare at the cross, out of breath, as though it's me who's been running. I stare at the cross and the crossroad that aren't supposed to be there then at my phone then back up again.

My foot's still flooring the pedal, I slowly lift it and feel the car moving forward, so I shift the gear into neutral and engage the handbrake. Only then do I sink into my seat a little. Just a moment. That's fine, I'm fine, my headlights are still on. I wanna close my eyes but it bothers me, it just does. I stare at the screen, and there's no crossroad on the screen, and maybe the whole thing's frozen, but granma's message came in just fine, and why does she care whether I've got my goddamn gri-gri—

I'm tired, I'm just really fucking tired. Do I have my gri-gri on? No the fuck I don't. I find the button and the window glides down, and I sit for a while, freezing, waking up, calming down. I'm in no hurry, after all. No the fuck I don't. I yank the glove compartment open and rummage without really looking. My palm and fingers find the necklace without meaning to. A damn ugly thing it is, that gri-gri. It's just a string with a clasp, and cat claws as pendants. I've been told those are Stripes's claws, I've been told Stripes liked to sleep on ma's pregnant belly, and in my cradle. She slept a lot and she hissed a lot, mostly at nothing, never at me. I don't remember, obviously, and I have no means to know where the claws really come from, obviously. I sigh, the necklace finds my neck.

The GPS app just isn't loading, I'm properly freezing. It's not good for the battery to keep the headlights on for so long. I'm pretty sure it'd be better to get a move on, in whichever direction. I start the engine and put the car in reverse to get a better look at my options. Who am I kidding, this is the middle of the woods. I drum my fingers on the wheel, I see a pair of eyes peeking at first, then approaching, moving along the ditch. Low to the ground, not a boar. A ball of white, spotted fur hops onto the road and trots into the halos of my headlights. Stops. The eyes blink.

'Polka?'

The ears move but not the body. Neutral, hand brake. Phone in pocket? Phone in pocket. I don't wanna get out, but I get out. Damn cat. Stripes's daughter or whatever stares, I don't know at what, I don't care at what. I walk past the point the road forks and the cross. There's no flowers, not that I assume it's a recent enough monument. But there's a crow that I hadn't noticed. It's big. Maybe a raven.

'Polka, you brat cat...'

I scoop her up easily, she doesn't have much to say for herself. I look at the road that forks into two, and back at the car, and behind it the fog that only seems to thicken. I can see my breath in the crisp air. There's that smell, that Berry smell. Granma used to say the fog and the smell were the witches' breaths. Granma still says that, actually. I start back for the car.

'Which's the way home, Polka?'

I thought she was purring, but she's rumbling, rumbling low, staring. I look at the cross, and the crow, but it's not a crow, it's a black hen. The black hen stares. Maybe I am in a hurry. I am, I have a strong sense that I am. I am. My phone vibrates in my pocket and the text says *Hurry home* I know it does without looking I just know and I jog back to the car and close the car door and put Polka in the passenger seat and I get the car moving I get it moving before I even have my seatbelt on and I take the road from which Polka walked and Polka hisses at the cross and the hen as we pass them but we pass them and she keeps hissing for a while, hissing at the backseat and I don't look, she hisses and I don't look, and then it's alright, she stops, it's alright.

The window's still open and I don't fumble in the dark for the button, I keep my two hands firmly on the wheel, and I drive. I drive, I don't try for the radio, either. Polka's not rumbling anymore, that's good. I wanna bury my face in my scarf and my body deep into my big girl leather coat but I can't, I drive. I'm all woken up. That's good.

The left hand clutches the wheel while I desperately try to refresh the app with the thumb of my right one. The text did say *Hurry home,* I don't spend too much brain power trying to understand that. I drop the phone onto my lap. I decide I'll drive down that road until I either end up at another crossroad or into some bit of civilisation, I decide that's a sensible decision.

The window's still open, the fresh air helps, it does. I think Polka is sleeping, she's all curled up, maybe she's cold. Maybe I should close the window, but the fresh air helps. I gotta stay awake?

Do I? I could stop on the side of the road, that wouldn't be so dangerous, given how few cars drive by. No cars, actually. I've seen no cars. That wouldn't be so bad, sleeping in the car. Wouldn't be so bad...

I am swallowed by a patch of fog, dense, so dense it's like driving in milk,

I barely slow down. I decide I trust my airbags.

I see it from faraway, I wanna pat myself on the back from seeing it from so far away. I don't wanna swerve, nor do I wanna honk, that doesn't feel like a good idea, making noise doesn't feel like a good idea. The deer doesn't move, it's staring at the car, staring at the headlights with wide eyes, wide dumb eyes, I slow down, I slow down a lot, shifting down gear after gear, but I don't stop and it doesn't move, it just doesn't, and I just, sorta bump into it with the front of my car. I bring the car to a stop, the deer barely stumbled back. I stare and it stares and I stare, gripping the wheel. I don't hear a single sound from Polka. And the deer drops to the ground.

I can see my breath and I can smell that smell. I should just roll over it, right? But it's alive, it's gotta be alive, it stared right at me, with wide dumb eyes, all white in the glare of my headlights. I look at Polka, she's asleep, or dead, or very calm. I look into the rearview mirror, and of course there's nothing. There are woods on either side of the road and no eyes, no pairs of eyes. I can almost hear the sound it would make, to roll over it, and I can't. I crack the door open, I step out. I don't dare to breathe. I get around to the front, the deer lies on the road, not quite in the middle, just in the way of my car. Unscathed. Do I speak to it?

I look over my shoulders. I swallow. I take a step forward, I touch the fur, little me always dreamed of touching the fur. The deer jolts awake, jolts up, stares at me, and I get a look at its eyes its real eyes without the glare and I shouldn't have done that.

I stare because I can't do much else and it stares because it needs me there it wants me there.

I see my breath I smell that smell and something is closing closing over and around me maybe it's the fog it's gotta be the fog.

Something behind me is certainly moving. It's steps it's not deer steps and it's not stag steps it's big it's big big big maybe boar maybe bear not human not human.

Polka's rumbling she's rumbling I don't know why I clutch the gri-gri around my neck and I shuffle back into the car I don't slam the door I don't know why but I don't I just close it I clutch it close.

I'm fine I'm fine I'm fine I have my big girl coat but Polka's rumbling and just put my other hand on her and she bites me but at least she shuts up.

I hear the steps. The deer still stares through the windshield with glaring eyes. I didn't make noise I didn't.

But

I'm

just

so

visible.

I clench my teeth. I let go of Polka and I flick the headlights off and I turn the key to stop the engine. There's darkness and there's silence. My hand finds Polka again and this time she wraps around it. She knows.

I squeeze my eyes shut because it doesn't make a difference. It's not a bear it's so much worse than a bear isn't it so so much worse than a bear.

I don't think about why a *deer* would wander alone during stag belling season and I don't think about the *deer's* eyes and how the pupils were split the wrong way.

I don't have a breath but I smell that smell and if I were breathing it'd burn my throat and make me cry. It's a witchcraft smell, it's a henhouse smell.

I don't think about how my window's still open. I clutch the door shut I don't think about how quick I could cramp. I don't I don't I don't.

The underwood gives under the steps it's massive it's so massive isn't it and it's walking it's massive and walking but it creaks it creaks like planks creak it creaks like a house a house a henhouse that reeks and creaks and walks.

It's going to pass me it's going to walk

past me but there's something else there's something else that I couldn't hear before. It's dragging itself there's dragging and then something hitting the underwood and then the asphalt and then dragging again and it goes on and on and that's how it moves and they move together and they're so fucking close.

I clench my teeth. I don't think about how the only thing between those and Polka and me is just a metal box on wheels and a gri-gri.

The dragging stops.

Something taps at my window. It's a branch and definitely not a nail.

Don't move don't look don't open your eyes don't breathe don't even exist just mind your non-existent business.

Something slides in fabric or old skin take your pick I can hear something sliding in because it makes the faintest sound against the glass and the smell fuck the smell.

It's in. Something's in.

It's hovering.

Mere inches away from my neck.

It slides out.

The dragging resumes.

I can't hold much more.

The dragging goes a bit faster than before because it needs to catch up probably. The steps fall over underwood again so it's on the other side of the road it's crossed it's going away it's going away.

I can't hold. I can't.

The dragging is still too close but the something that hits the asphalt now hits the underwood again.

I can't hold but I'd rather die suffocating.

Almost gone, almost gone.

My phone vibrates.

Dinner's ready.

I whimper and gasp for air and the steps and the dragging stop.

I don't open my eyes I just slam that damn door and turn the ignition and shift the gear and for a moment the car doesn't move and just roars and fuck the hand brake and I release the hand brake and the car just fucking *goes*.

And I drive and I drive and I don't have my headlights on and I don't fucking care I just drive I drive so fast I can't hear anything else but the engine and I

don't

look

back.

Granma welcomes me home with fresh bread and a warm dinner and a warm blanket and she's so glad I brought back Polka and I'm so glad she's not dead and also that she told me to wear my gri-gri.

COUNT POLLEN

BARRY CHARMAN

Aye, Count Pollen they call him. Tall figure of a man, glimpsed across the hills, walking swiftly through the crops. Folk tales? Oh God yes, how long have you got? They say if you sneeze you've got twenty four hours before he kills you. They say he takes your blood and uses it to water his crops. What crops are these? You make me laugh, dear. I can't say, and I don't think I'd like to speculate, not got that kind of mind, y'see.

✦✦✦

What's that? Count Pollen? Ah now. Aint heard that name in— but why you askin' bout that? Nice girl like you. Be off with you. Troubling little old ladies— don't matter what you meant, *harm comes from no harm meant*. That's as true as anything you'll ever hear. Look at me, crossing myself. That's on you, girl.

✦✦✦

Any county as old as this has its odd tales and myths, all mixed in its history. Weird, vivid, quaint. I thought they should be re-membered, preserved. My teacher told me; *'when you graduate, you have to stop waiting for the world to come to you, you have to go and meet it.' So I did.*

People don't like to talk, but stories are waiting to be written.

✦✦✦

Let me think. Aye, name does ring some bells. Ye want to speak to Timothy, really, *the mad boy*. Oh, don't look like that; he's no boy now, not mad neither. We used to call him that when we were kids. God, we were little bastards. Did we throw rocks at him...? Think we did, can't swear to it. Why? Cos we didn't want to listen, and he wouldn't stop talking. Just wouldn't stop talking.

✦✦✦

The mad boy? Lord as my witness, not been called *that* in a few years I've not. Who've you been talking to, eh? Count Pollen? What do you want to be writing about him for? That aint a knowledge of the world to *keep*. Oh, oh I don't know that I should talk about... Talking did never do me any good. Not been seen has he, not for how long? Tall thing, he was, I always saw him as a spider standing up. Did awful drawings, I did. Black crayons and red. Yellow for a moon full of pus... Baleful witness... What did he do? Just walk with that purpose of his. Midsummer he would be about. Walked like a scythe, cutting people dead. Aye, I saw that too, but I won't talk 'bout it, not to no one.

✦✦✦

Ridiculous! Yes, I've heard about him. Usually makes an appearance after a few ales. Nothing can't be explained by a couple of lads putting their heads together. People go off in the woods and mess about. Animals do things to other animals to mark their territory. Nature's a bitch. Keeps a tally. Wants to keep the land red. All the things that drive you younguns out your skull; all *natural*, all of it. All of it.

✦✦✦

I'd first heard of the Count whispered in a smoky corner of a dim bar I knew I never wanted to go back to. The whole thing was wonderfully peculiar, and I realised he'd gone entirely undocumented. So I followed the story from person to person, everyone had a piece of a puzzle no one wanted to look at.
Amazing.

✦✦✦

Well, I got this stump from out in the fields, few summers back. Cut the tree down, diseased you see, but there were no rings inside it. Just these scratch marks. Little crosses, some say. Devilry. Not saying the Count's some devil, but then I'm not saying he's a real Count either! Around the tree? Oh everything was dead. Whole crop gone. That was the year of the bone wheat. That's what they called it in these parts. It were *hard*, you see, like it were stone, or *worse*. Dig? No, we didn't *dig*... You should go now, love.

Never heard of no Count. But there was a feller, young man. He was painting the area. Loved the fields. Said *It's not Constable country, but it's close.* Nice lad. Always saw him around the place. Easel under his arm, big bag of paints. He came back from some place one day, had a strange look about him. Always loved to show off his landscapes, used to sell a few down at the pub, but he wouldn't show them anymore.

I remember he seemed scared to go back out there. In the end he had to down a few for courage first. Then, of course, his paintings weren't so good. That angered him, I think. He went off to this old field he'd found—though it didn't sound proper, not the way he described it—and he just never came back. Still remember the look on his face. A man who didn't want to put paint down no more, but couldn't accept it. Frightened. But some folk just are. The country's too quiet for them. City folk. The silence floods into them, and they're not ready.

Where do I think he went? Oh, he just walked into some landscape and never found his way out. Happens, I imagine.

✦✦✦

Paintings, dear? Oh yes. Lovely things. He was such a bright young man. Really *saw* the world clearly. Not everyone does, I assure you. Why certainly I could show you— Oh, one of his later ones? Ah. Ah, no. I didn't like them. Not at *all*. Didn't buy any, I don't think he was selling them either. Not the land I recognised. Not the waking land, that.

What do I mean? Doesn't matter, dear. Doesn't stand up to thinking about.

✦✦✦

David Lewis. Twenty seven. Studied

*fine art at Brighton. Got a BA. Had a
thousand canvases ahead of him. Went
missing over a year ago. They happen
sporadically. Enough for tales to get tall,
but not often enough for people to get
worried. To do anything. But then people
just go missing don't they? The world
eats them up, and we shrug it off.*

*But the people who go missing here,
never turn up again. No bodies. No
trace.*

Just the stories they leave behind.

✦✦✦

I've heard about you— I don't got
nothing to say— no! Just leave me be.
People should have more sense then be
talking about things they don't know
nothin' about. All you need know girl, is if
you don't see the devil, he don't see you.
Think on that. Just you think on that.

✦✦✦

Did I see him? Ah now. Ah now. I
were a girl. Just a wee girl. We were in
the fields one day. I thought I saw a tree
walking towards me... Mama sneezed.
There was a wind; the blossom was
blown across the fields, like a low cloud.
A tall man was upon us. Had a face like a
dead flower. I saw him closer than most,
I s'pose. No, I didn't lose my sight just
then, that was next morning. Why did it
happen? God's will. I can't see him, not
anymore, but I can dream of *her* every
night. God is full of love.

✦✦✦

Well, on one hand it's a joke, isn't
it? I mean, *Count Pollen!* But there *was*
an old house up in the moors. Burned
down. Couldn't even tell you when. Man
who built that must have been *somebody*
though. Every county had a Count, once.
Records? That far back? Maybe...
Aye, you might stir something.

But you're stirring ashes. Just so you know.

+++

The old house? Aye, just follow the old dirt road. Go past the wheat till nothing grows, wait till the road turns to cracks. Oh, I've heard the tales, sure enough. Mother told me what her mother told her. Some say there was a German, he disgraced a noble house and was sent to live here. Had an honorary title back home, yet he was given a house made of rubble to lord over. Raged, he did. Wandered worse than any cloud. Tried to make a success of himself, but his crop— Well, he never grew anything that lived. Make of that what you will. The devil did.

+++

So the stories took me to what was left of the old house. God, what a place. Never seen stone burnt black. I've never felt such silence. Like something's holding its breath. I cut through a field full of black flowers, all curled up like little hands. So deserted, so peaceful... But then I thought I saw something— thought it was a crooked tree, but it was beckoning...Gone when I turned back, though. I'm going to look at what's left of the house. Feel like it's looking at me. Blinking.

+++

I can't find the road, and I don't want to turn around. I can hear the season turning in my footsteps. Can feel fingers raking down the back of my neck.
Feel so stupid writing this, but I love you mum, I love everyone. xxx.

+++

I'll be laughing about this tomorrow. Nothing here but what I brought. But just in case. If anyone finds this— Don't come here. Don't look. Don't go inside. Let stories fade. They can diminish like that. Leave shadows with nothing to harvest.
I'll start.
There is nothing behind me. There is nothing behind me. There is n

+++

(Pages found pinned to a tree in an untended field, author unknown.)

F LOCAL AGENT...

PPIN & WEBB,
Travelling Bags
FOR
Ladies and Gentlemen.
Best Materials and Workmanship.
Illustrated Catalogue free.

MAPPIN & WEBB,
Oxford Street (76, 77, and 78), W.;
AND
Queen Victoria Street (No. 2), City,
London.

JOHN W...

EXTRA
GLACÉ COTTON
CROCHET OR
TATTING COTTON.
In Skeins or on Reels.
Unsurpassed in Quality.

J & P COAT

SIX CORD

COTTO

Obtained the only
Award at the
Philadelphia Exhi-
bition, 1876. For
superior strength
and excellent
quality.

BENT WOOD FURNITURE.
THONET BROTHERS,
VIENNA,
ORIGINAL INVENTORS AND
MANUFACTURERS OF THE ABOVE.
The strongest, most durable, and best finished goods
ever yet produced, combining lightness and elegance with
very moderate cost. Suitable for the cottage or mansion.
London Depot: 125, HIGH HOLBORN.
DEPÔTS:
BUDAPEST, BRÜNN, PRAGUE, GRAZ, PARIS,
HAMBOURG, BRUSSELS, MILAN, NAPLES,
NEW YORK, CHICAGO, &c.
Book of Designs and Price List free per post.
Prize Medals and Awards: London, 1851, 1862; Paris, 1855, 1867;
Stettin, 1865; Hamburg, 1862; Cassel, 1870: Jurors, Exhibition,
Vienna, 1873; Philadelphia, 1876, &c.

LAV

THE
Much
LA

POST FREE O
Every Article Warranted,

'S COAL TAR SOAP.
FAMILY of DISTINCTION in the CIVILISED WORLD.
It is the most Health-preserving adjunct to the
Toilet ever discovered. Acknowledged and recom-
mended by all the leading Medical Journals and the
highest authorities in the medical profession. Vide
Testimonials.
"It is the only true antiseptic soap."—*British*
Medical Journal.
"In our hands it has been most effective in skin
diseases."—*Lancet.*
"An unfailing remedy for unpleasant emanations
from the person.—*Medical Times.*
Invented and Introduced by the Sole Proprietors,
W. V. WRIGHT and CO., London,
Proprietors of the COAL TAR PILL (*Pilule*
Carbonis Detergens) and SOLUTION OF
COAL TAR (*Liquor Carbonis Detergens*) par-
ticulars of which accompany each tablet of the
Coal Tar Soap.
he impress "SAPO CARBONIS DETERGENS."

CAUTION.—Each Tablet of the genuine Soap be

SINCE THE ISSUE OF OUR
ILLUSTRATED FUR
the applications for Copies have become
a small nominal charge of 2s. each for
the cost, and heavy postage. We are
they receiving such a large number of
numerous instances from parties in the
furnishing or purchasing.
Those parties who pay for the Cat
however small the extent, may deduct

MRS. STEVENS
30, MARKHAM SQUARE
COURT MILLINER AND DRESS
PUNCTUALITY AND MODERATE
LADIES' OWN MATERIALS
Special Department for the Altera
Dresses to the Existing Fa
NOVELTIES IN DRESSIN
Mantles, Jackets, C
MOURNING AND WEDDING OR
ON THE SHORTEST
Millinery of all De

THE GUN OF TH
Has carried the Hono
Exhibition,

ON SALE ALL THE YEAR ROUND.
ROYAL DEVONSHIRE SERGE,
MADE OF SELECTED AND ELASTIC STAPLE WOOLS.
No other Article manufactured equals this in general utility.
It is Woven for LADIES' DRESSES in Navy Blue and other Solid Colours, and
in Heather or Homespun Mixtures, price 1s. 11d., 2s. 6d., and 2s. 11d. per yard; also
in LIGHT-WEIGHTED YARNS for SUMMER USE. And for Children's
Wear, in White and Navy Blue, at 1s. 6½d. per yard. The qualities for Boys' Hard Wear
are extra Milled and Strengthened, as also those for Gentlemen's Suits; prices, 54 in. wide,
from 4s. 9d. per yard.
BOOKS of PATTERNS will be sent on application to
SPEARMAN and SPEARMAN,
DEVONSHIRE SERGE FACTORS, PLYMOUTH.
The ROYAL DEVON SERGE is the only true Yachting Serge. Sea-
...e it. Good Wear is positively guaranteed by the Factors, who cut any
...riage to London, whence Parcels are cheaply distributed through-

WHISKY

A DEATH IN THE FAMILY

MAUD WOOLF

This morning when she wakes up and creeps downstairs, holding her breath and stepping around the creaks, Winona finds the front door will not open. She stands by it in her dressing gown, at first moving the handle softly and then, when the panic rises in a white prickle, rattling it, yanking and pulling and pleading softly until her hand aches and holds a slicing red imprint of metal across the palm.

When she realises there is nothing she can do she goes into the kitchen and finds her mother sitting at the table with all the tea things spread out in front of her, the willow pattern and teaspoons and the heavy metal pot they inherited from a distant great-aunt.

'The door is locked,' Winona says.

'It's always been locked,' says her mother. 'Have some tea.'

Winona sits down and when the tea is poured she takes a sip and finds it ice-cold. She drinks deeply, anyway, greedily, through chapped and breaking lips. She's so thirsty. How long has she slept this time?

They sit there in silence for a while and Winona is grateful for it but all too soon her mother puts down her cup and starts up again with her questions, the questions that make Winona want to grit her teeth and rock back and forth and put her hands over her ears.

'Where is Loop? Where is Carina? Are they safe? Are they eating?'

'They're fine mum,' Winona says and she's said it so many times now. 'They're fine, they're upstairs, you can go and see them.'

For a moment it seems as though for once her mother will listen, that this will work, but then it comes again, that awful racking hacking cough from above and they both still, barely breathing, their necks craned back to look at the water-stained ceiling.

Her mother lets out a long and rattling breath. 'He's awake again. Oh god. He's awake.'

'Why didn't he unlock the door?' Winona asks. 'He always unlocks it in the morning.'

'It was always locked. Don't go upstairs.'

'I won't,' Winona promises but she has to, they both know that, and so she gets up and kisses her mother goodbye on the top of her head. The white fine hairs are almost transparent over the hard ridge of the skull below. Her mother's dress has the same pattern as the wallpaper and it grows and grows by the day, swallowing up her mother's brittle wrists and legs and neck.

At the bottom of the stairs Winona hesitates, looking again over at the door. Her mother was right. It had always been locked but how could that be true?

For not too long ago she had walked in through that door, Winona's almost sure of that. Loop had opened it for her and they had held each other tightly for a long time, Loop boney and red-eyed and smelling, as always, very strongly of dog.

And Winona had forgotten a bag in her car and, going back to get it, she had looked over her shoulder at the house and been struck suddenly thinking of when they were children, thinking of years and years ago, when she had looked at the house with a child's eyes and seen the four front-facing windows, one for each of them: her mother and her sisters and her. And she had thought, where was my father in the neat little face of this house? And she had remembered that he was the door, that he had always been the door, shut tight and keeping out all of the danger, keeping them safe inside.

Now Winona hears again the coughing from upstairs and she puts her hand on the bannister to steady herself.

'I'm coming!' she calls up. 'Just a moment!'

The stairway is lined with photographs, generations stretching back and back, each more alien than the last. When they were younger she and her sisters had sat on the stairway, one two three in order of age and looked for themselves in the dead faces. Auntie Jean looks like you, Loop had told Carina and Carina had cried because Auntie Jean had a pug's scrunched up face resting on her starched collar.

Carina was always crying, she was the baby of the family. She cried when her pet rabbit died and when Winona left for university but also for silly things like rain falling on a picnic day and people being a little too late to call her back. Carina cried all the time but she had not been crying on the day that Winona had come back to the house. She had cleaned and cooked and watched television too loudly and listened to music too loudly and hummed and breathed and talked too loudly and Winona had wished for once that Carina could be still and quiet. And the rest of them, her mother and Loop and Winona, had sat on the sofa, mute with grief while Carina chattered and chattered and chattered.

Carina makes everything about herself, Loop had said. She thinks this is just her tragedy. She thinks she's being so brave.

Winona takes one step and another and by the third it has become a familiar rolling motion and almost easy. At the landing she turns and smells all at once, the stink of wet fur, the smoke that spills out from under Loop's bedroom door.

It occurs to Winona that Loop has not come out in a long time. Perhaps her dogs have eaten her.

This is something Winona was always afraid of. Loop is tall like her but so thin, thin in a way that Winona once obsessed over, thin in a way that was effortless. Winona had spent her childhood measuring her own chubby thighs and arms against the long lean stretch of Loop but when Winona had returned home, it had for the first time been frightening. Frightening to see Loop's head wobbling on top of her long neck, surrounded by her leaping, noisy pack. The way Loop's dogs loved her was frightening too. Hungry. The silent hulking German shepherd, the manic Pomeranian, the tragic Schnauzer, and neurotic, damaged mongrel. Winona knew there would hardly be enough of Loop's frail body to give any of them more than a mouthful each. When they barked at Loop she barked right back into their toothy, froth-flecked snouts.

It had been Loop who had discovered that first night that the door was locked. She had been going out to smoke.

And that was right, Winona thinks, grasping eagerly at the memory. The door had only been locked at night. Just like when they were children. To keep them safe.

But when she told Loop that, Loop had been so angry. Why? Winona wonders now.

Perhaps because their father had always been the one to lock the door. And Loop had said that it was impossible, that he was too sick, that he couldn't move from his bed. But still, when Winona went upstairs into that room filled with soft beeping machines and wires, and reached under her father's pillow (his head had been so light, nothing more than a hard skull under soft fine white hairs), her fingers had closed around the key.

As she passes Loop's door now Winona wonders if she should knock. But Loop would only tell her to go away, Loop has always told people to go away, as a stubborn middle child, as a distraught messy teenager, as a lonely adult. Winona puts her hand to the door, smelling again the cigarettes, the animals and struggles for a moment, wondering which Loop is waiting there in the darkness.

How old is she now? Thirty? Four years younger than Winona, who had named her, who had not been able to pronounce Calliope.

Their father had wanted to give them all unique, special names, names that would set them apart. And it had. Too much. One little push and the door swings open, letting out a rush of warm, stinking air and also, cacophony. The dogs are angry. They don't like to be disturbed. Loop never likes to be disturbed. Do they sound hungry? There is more of

Winona to go around. She shuts the door tight again, moves on.

The next room on the landing is her's but Winona knows what is inside. A suitcase spilling out dirty clothes. An unopened laptop full of unread emails. She had packed in a rush when she had heard the call, not brought much. She had only meant to stay a week, her mother had said there wasn't much time left. A few days, the doctor said and then of course, the organisation, the paperwork, the funeral. How long ago was that?

The coughing again. 'Hold on,' she tries to shout and the words fall out as shrivelled little leaves.

Only a few days, the doctor said, but a week into the waiting and he had not died.

This house is too tall, too narrow. Winona has to squeeze herself up the next flight of stairs, pressing her back to wallpaper the colour of her mother's dress. The dogs are still barking behind her but they are not frightening anymore, not as frightening as the silence above. Because the silence can, could be, will be broken again.

It was broken that first night they had all slept here, as Winona stayed up late, hunched over her laptop in bed in a soft-blue bubble of light. Answering emails, soothed by mindless routine, she had heard it, the creak of the stairs outside. The footsteps.

And she had thought, it's just Carina, she's finally going to bed. And she had thought, this house has always made noises. And she had thought, it is getting closer, it has its hand on my door, he knows I am listening. And she had closed the laptop, pulled the covers over her head and waited in the dark, holding her breath until the footsteps went away.

Maybe the house has not always been this small, maybe it is shrinking or maybe Winona is just getting larger and larger. They say everything is different when you come back to your childhood house. They say you can't go home again but maybe they mean you shouldn't, maybe they mean don't, it's not safe.

Winona has to duck her head on the landing, hands feeling her way through the dark. There was once a skylight here but her mother has taped it over because her father couldn't sleep with the light, and all he does now is sleep, sleep with his eyes flicking under the lids, sleep with spit dribbling down his chin. Sleep and sleep and when he isn't sleeping he eats.

On the first night their mother had served them pasta and on the second, pie. On the third she had brought out a great pot of soup and Carina had taken off the lid and ladled out a bowl of cold grey dishwasher. Scum had been floating on the surface and Winona had tried to understand but she could not. Loop had tried to laugh and she could not and Carina had laid a hand on their mother's arm and asked her gently what it meant, if it meant anything?

He's doing it again, their mother had said, he's trying to make me look crazy.

They had all surrounded her, cooing and soft and reasonable, saying, no, saying, how could he, bed-ridden, insensible, upstairs?

And then on the fourth night he had come down to join them for supper.

The coughing again, wretched, resentful and Winona holds her hands to her ears, muttering, 'I'm coming, I'm coming, hold on, please.'

And then she shouts it, voice catching painfully in her throat, 'Just wait, just wait a moment!'

She will ask him why the door is locked. Maybe today she will be brave enough to reach under the pillow again, mindful of his gnashing, snarling mouth (all the teeth had grown back now, popping up in his mouth like wet little pebbles).

When he had eaten with them that night, there had been nothing but pink gums but that hadn't stopped him, that only made it easier for him to slurp and guzzle his way through chicken and mashed potatoes and gravy. He had been so hungry, ravenous, buttering slice after slice of bread and licking at the knife. He had eaten his serving and then another and then Carina's and their mother's and still it wasn't enough. He asked for pudding, he asked for wine and cheese and coffee.

They had brought it to him, silently, getting up one by one to go to the kitchen. They couldn't talk; what could they say? That they were happy to see him feeling better? All of them knew, even then, he was not better, he was not well. He was something else and growing stronger.

When at last he was finished, he wiped his mouth with the tablecloth and smiled and opened his mouth but did not speak. They all heard the words anyway, bubbling up from the primordial ooze of the past.

All my girls in one place. What a lucky man I am.

Loop had gathered her pack around her and slunk back into her smokey cave and their mother had sat at the kitchen table shrinking away into her dress and Carina....

Oh god, Winona thinks now, clutching at the wall, hearing the drip drip drip from behind the bathroom door ahead of her. Carina.

The coughing again, so close now it rattles the bannister under her hand and Winona wishes that someone else could take her place, anyone else.

Winona is the eldest daughter. The responsibility falls, as it always had, to her. So she goes upstairs every day to bring him down, to sit him at the table and bring out the food, to listen to the sounds he makes. She takes him upstairs when he is satisfied and puts him back

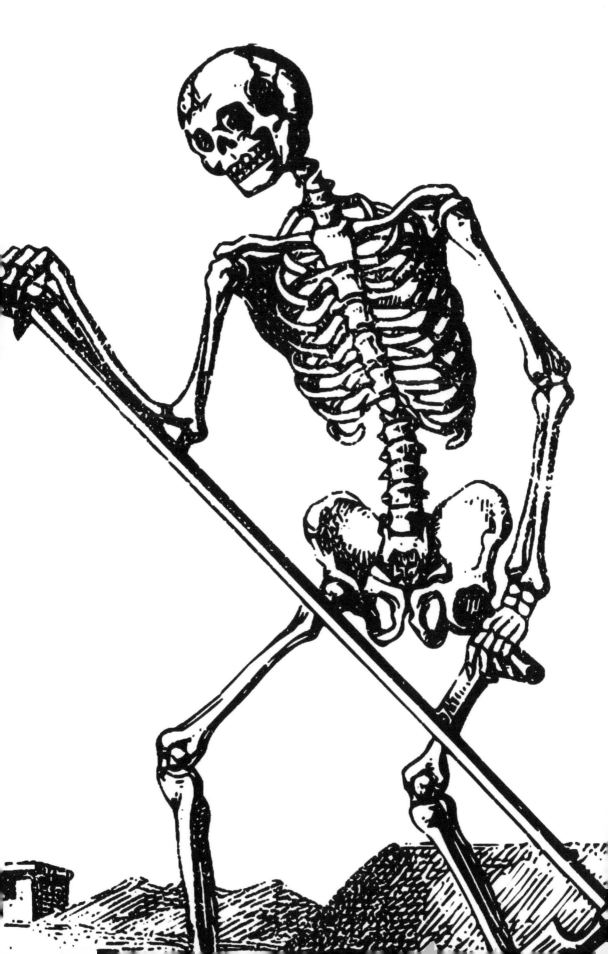

in bed, nestled among all the dead and dusty machinery. All useless now and defunct, the wires spooled limp on the carpet.

He does not need them anymore. He has found an alternative and he's greedy for it, he takes and takes and takes.

Carina, Winona thinks again, hand on the bathroom door now, too scared to look inside. Carina what do you look like now? Are you still in the bathtub? Is the water not very cold?

She wants to open the door but the thought of Carina, waterlogged and wrinkled, stops her. Carina had come home with blue hair and red hair and pink, but on that first night it had been green and Winona had tugged gently at the ends of it and said, mermaid.

And Carina had grinned and chattered and cleaned and sung and, under her mascaraed eyes the black bruises spread, because she was not sleeping, she had not slept for days. At night she hunched in on herself on the couch, red eyes fixed on late night television and when Winona came downstairs and asked, were you walking around last night? Carina had said no.

She had said the same thing the next morning and the next and then Winona had stopped asking and then he had come downstairs for dinner and as they were clearing away the dishes and he was asking for more, Carina had put her head down on the tablecloth and closed her eyes. Winona and Ruth had taken her to bed and brushed the crumbs out of her hair, the salt and pepper and small soft fragments of cake.

The more their father woke the more Carina slept, and when she was not sleeping in her bed she went to the bathroom and locked the door tight and slept in the bathtub with the steam cooling into mist above her. Maybe that green hair was drifting now, like seaweed, or maybe it had risen, clotted to the surface, mildewy scum on a lake. Winona presses her ear to the door, holds her breath and then she hears it, a faint splashing and that's enough, enough to let that treacherous thought bubble up. Perhaps it's not too late.

The coughing is so loud now that her father's door is straining at its hinges, the floor is shaking beneath Winona's feet so violently she thinks perhaps the house will fall in around them, bury them all here, perhaps that's what he wants.

Perhaps Winona wants that too, but still, because she has to, because she was always going to and always will, because she has no choice, she opens the door.

Then everything, the coughing, the noise, the impending destruction, stops.

There is quiet.

The sound of breathing.

He has been waiting for her. He smiles. His hair is thick and dark against the white pillow.

As Winona helps him up, uselessly, out of habit, out of ritual, her hand slips beneath the pillow and for a moment his grip on her tightens. There is nothing there and when she looks at him, at the clear glitter of his eyes, at the white gravestone slabs of his teeth as he grins, she realises what has happened to the key. He has eaten it. He's so hungry these days.

As they make their way downstairs, slowly, carefully, Winona feels the emptiness beneath her ribs and knows she cannot blame him.

They are, all three of them, their father's daughters. He was not dead and there had been no reading of the will, but here it is, their inheritance. Carina's wrinkling weakened body, Loop's bitter snarling rage but, as the oldest daughter, the lion's share is Winona's. She takes the brunt of the birthright: she has his appetite.

His head brushes just below the ceiling but unlike Winona, he does not stoop. The house inhales and expands to let him through. Winona's steps falter in the dark but he guides her, her father. Her hand feels very small in his. The dogs are silent as they pass.

Downstairs in the dining room, he takes his place at the head of the table and waits to see what his daughter will bring him.

She retreats to the kitchen, where her mother has disappeared completely into the wallpaper. The teacups, the pot, sit orphaned on the kitchen table. Winona looks away from them, to the cupboards. What was left now? What had they managed to hide?

Stiffly, methodically, belly-aching she makes a meal from dusty old cans of vegetables, the shrink-wrapped meats hiding in the bottom of the refrigerator, frost-furred. Most of what she finds is old, rotting and soured, but that's alright: she will cover the taste with spices, with gravy and salt. Whatever will cover the taste of bleach, antifreeze, ammonia and whatever else she can find beneath the sink. She sprinkles careful handfuls of rat poison into the tomato sauce, seasons every cutlet with a spray of air freshener. As she cooks, she moves faster and faster, hands slipping on the knife as she chops up yellowing broccoli and tosses it in the pot of boiling water and drain cleaner. Her bare hands are raw with chemicals; her mouth waters. She's so hungry. She should have done this long ago but even yesterday it had been unthinkable. Even today, right now, it is unthinkable. She does not think: she cooks instead and when it is ready she brings it out, dish by steaming dish and sets the table. When this is over, the door may unlock. It may have always been unlocked.

A plate in front of him, a fork, two knives. He does not eat. He looks at the empty chair beside him. Winona sets herself a place. She fills his plate. Still he does not move.

The food is cooling between them. Winona can smell the chemicals settling in the air between them, a miasma. Her father speaks.

'Eat with me,' he says and Winona wonders, is that concern on his face?

He loves me, she thinks, he won't let me go hungry. I love him, he won't starve.

She lifts her fork and he does the same. They are just reflections of each other. They say you can't go home again. They say you cannot leave. They say you will carry it with you, always, on your back. In your stomach.

She takes a bite and, watching her, trusting her, he does the same.

They eat. They eat. They eat.

THE OLD MAN

ELIN OLAUSSON

Things happened to Marla's eyesight after she started visiting the old man in the woods. Not necessarily bad things, not to begin with. Just changes, and change was the reason she visited the old man in the first place. Everyone had their reasons, and this was her's—the cramps, the blood, the swelling in unwanted places. Life had been much simpler before and she wished for it to take a turn, or two, or however many were necessary to whirl back in time. The old man put his hand on her forehead and sang in that voice that wasn't a voice at all, and on the way home Marla thought that the woods looked different. She visited him seven times before realising why. There was a juniper tree beside the path, and Marla used to stop and pick a berry whenever she passed it. The berries stung her tongue, sharp and bitter like the old man's eyes, and she ate them to ward off his smell and his ancient soul. They were a deep, bluish colour, like the shadows haunting the old man's face.

This time, that colour was gone. The berries hung lifeless, grey; she had to squint to make them out. She craned her neck, twisted her head. It didn't matter. The juniper berries had lost their shine, and she came home to find that the bruise on her mother's arm had faded, too. As if that certain shadow-blue was

gone forever, and she could never have it back.

After that, she realised that she'd lost other colours as well. The deep sea-green of her favourite dress; the dreamish grey eyes of the newborn baby next door; the soft pink whispers on the underside of the begonia leaves. She asked her mother to see if her world had changed, too, but her frown told Marla all she needed to know. It was her, only her, and it was because of the old man in the woods.

She asked him about it a week later, after she'd lost the lilacs and the peonies and the edges of the rainbow. He put his hand on her forehead and sang, and the change ran through her. When she came home she bit into an apple, ash-grey and sour, and her mother said she looked as thin as a bean stalk.

'It's unnatural,' she said. 'It's unnatural, what you're doing.'

But Marla didn't stop visiting the old man. She sank down at his feet, because there was no other place for her to sit, and she was tired. He put his hand on her head and drained her of colour, fat, and blood.

'Tell me a story,' she asked him. 'Tell me about births and passings, about silver and gold.'

The old man laughed. He sang in that language that was nothing like her's, and his grave-deep voice shimmered with precious metals. Marla came home to find her father's wedding bands in their usual spot on top of the dresser. They were lifeless, robbed of their shine, and the old man's laughter skipped through her head like a playing child.

✦✦✦

Her brother followed her into the woods one night, as brothers do. Marla's shadow had narrowed just like her body, but her brother had no shadow at all and she didn't see him. Even while looking straight at him, she sometimes forgot about his existence—she had lost the sandiness of his hair, the cat-glow of his eyes. She went into the woods without thinking about Little Brother, and the old man sang, and the yellow of buttercups fell from her sight into his waiting hands.

Little Brother blocked her path on the way home. Marla saw him as a trick of the light, a ripple of fear and anger among the beeches.

'I want you to be like you were before. Not like this.'

Marla laughed, because he was small and foolish and his colours were all wrong. 'People change, Little Brother. It's the way of the world, and it always has been.'

'Mama says you're turning into a bean stalk. One day we'll look for you everywhere, and you won't be around.'

'She doesn't know any more than you do.' Marla pushed him aside and walked on, past the juniper tree that was barely visible to her now, its greens gone just like the blue shade of the berries. She couldn't remember what those berries had tasted like, or why she had forced herself to eat them.

'Why do you go into the woods?' Little Brother called after her. 'Why do your eyes look different?'

In her room that night, Marla watched her face in the mirror. It was gaunt and ghostly, and she loved it so much that she had no time to search her eyes for any changes.

✦✦✦

The girls who had used to be her friends twirled through the village like fallen leaves, draped in colours she couldn't see. Marla sat on the floor beneath the window and listened to their laughter, and to the boys' names that dropped like birdseeds to the ground. She had been like them, a flare of light, until her body betrayed her and she was weighed down. She had collected boys' names like sapphires, and boys' smiles like ancient diamonds. Eli, Graham, Louis. They had all gathered by the river on slow summer nights, mouths tasting like beer and sundown, and Marla had lowered her face close to the water and watched her skin, her eyes, her grinning mouth. Eli had kissed her, then Graham, then Louis. The girls had sung and she had joined in, believing that she would stay the same forever. When the first changes rippled through her, she pretended not to notice. Everyone else became better, prettier, more defined, as if adulthood was all gloss and shine. Marla didn't become anything. Her new face was blotchy, covered in pimples that burst and left her scarred. None of her silky dresses fit her widening hips, and the boys leered at the lumps growing on her chest, their smiles nothing like precious gems. She cried the first time she bled, and when her mother explained for how long the bleeding would continue she cried more. There were no more nights by the river, because the old Marla was gone and someone new had taken over her body. She started dressing in black, in heavy fabrics that swallowed her and blurred her out.

'Why don't you ever invite your friends over anymore?' her mother had asked, as if she didn't know. As if she didn't notice that Marla had turned into something different, something that no one wanted to

be friends with.

But it was from the other girls that she had found out about the old man in the woods. They had whispered to each other during class, their voices like tiny birds whirring over Marla's head.

'Did you hear that Lara Eve got pregnant?'

The air electrified with girl-giggles. Lara Eve was three years older, with a bearded boyfriend and skin that smelled like rose petals.

'But she went to the old man, and he got rid of it for her.'

Marla had watched the teacher draw chalk lines on the blackboard, but she didn't hear anything except the hushed voices around her.

'Who is he? How long has he been out there?'

They had stopped giggling. Their silence reminded Marla that they were all little girls just like her, and there were things that scared them.

'No one knows. But he can sense what you need, and he'll give it to you. If you dare to seek him out.'

'Is he dangerous?' a voice had said. Marla was shocked when she realised it was her own.

The girls had been silent around her, shifting uncomfortably in their seats. Their eyes burned her and she knew they were all thinking about how ugly she had become.

'Only if you've got something to lose,'

one of them had answered her question. In that moment, Marla knew what she had to do.

✦✦✦

She kept visiting the old man every night, while her family were having supper at the oaken table, beeswax candles sweetening the air. Marla dropped to the ground at the old man's feet, and he sang about darkness and greed. His hands touched her hair and face, and she smiled because her cheeks were hollows for his fingertips to bury themselves in. On the way back she had to walk slowly, because her head felt light and her field of vision was swarming with blacks and greys and little else. She sensed shapes moving around her, hands landing on her arms and shoulders. But they were not the hands of the old man, and she shrugged them off.

She went into the woods for the last time the next evening. Her surroundings had turned to mud. Gone were the cramps, the blood, and the swelling in unwanted places. Gone were the berries, the apples, and the edges of the rainbow. She stumbled into the woods, thin as a bean stalk, and fell to the old man's feet. He grabbed her head and started singing, his voice piercing her skin. Marla turned her head up to look into his eyes, his ancient eyes that knew everything about her, and her world went black.

COMING OR GOING

DAVID TOWSEY

Martin's grip was too tight, too tight and too sweaty. Chloe tried to wriggle free but, when they were on the platform, it was no good. He pulled her along, looking bigger and wider than ever against the grey sky. The clouds weren't rain clouds, which was kind of lucky because Chloe's raincoat was at the bottom of her rucksack. And the hood had holes in it from the last time it rained.

Martin started up his usual huffing and puffing as they passed bench after empty bench. The man was muttering but Chloe couldn't hear if he was using any naughty words, so instead she counted. Five, four, three, and the lights flickered on; she'd misjudged them again. Their pale, sickly yellow did little to help the gloom on the platform, and made Martin's greasy hair look even more sad.

'Here we are,' Martin said as they came to the seventh bench, their bench. The other benches were fine but this was his way. He let go without looking at her and sat down. He crossed his arms in his big old army coat; it wasn't a raincoat but it did have holes, he'd just patched them. With her help, of course.

Chloe scuffed her trainers on the tight concrete of the platform, all kickable stones long gone. Her rucksack weighed heavy on her shoulders, but he wouldn't let her take it off, not before the train.

'Chips for tea tonight, is it?' he said with a small smile.

She nodded. 'Little gravy. In the corner.'

'Bit of fish?' he asked.

But Chloe was distracted by something moving at the far end of the platform, out where the concrete met the weeds. A flash of grubby white. Some part of her knew what it was, a memory she couldn't place, not specifically, and that it was something rare now. She was inching towards it without really meaning to.

'Bit of fish?' Martin said, starting to sound desperate.

'Not for me,' she said.

'No, me neither.'

He was smiling again as the newspaper tumbled along the tracks and out of sight. Chloe sighed and sat beside him, swinging her legs and trying to ignore the odd feeling of the missing slat in the bench.

It got proper dark without her noticing. The light above them was full of dead insects, but she could still see Martin starting to sweat. He wiped at the beads running down his face.

'Bit of fish?' he said when he noticed her

looking at him.

She shook her head. He glared at her until she said it. 'Not for me.'

'No, me neither.'

The bell started to ring. Where it was, she couldn't say; it seemed to come from all across the platforms. She knew better than to stand up. Instead, she peered past Martin's belly and the folds of his big coat, down the track towards the growing light of the train. The ringing stopped and for a few long minutes there was no sound except Martin's wheezing. Then the train came. Something in her stirred at the noise of it and she wanted, for a moment, to get up and dance.

She wasn't supposed to look at the front of the train as it rumbled by. Martin didn't like the way the plating and the plough was like a nasty helmet, said it reminded him of bad times. And not all the red that coloured that helmet was paint; Chloe knew what the stains were, and they didn't come out easily.

The train took its time stopping. The front and the engine were a long way down the platform now, but that wasn't why Martin had led them to the seventh bench.

Where they waited, a heavy door opened. Metal steps led high into the carriage and she couldn't see what was beyond. She waited. The train settled a little on the tracks, taking a breather, which was why she could hear Martin.

'No,' he muttered. He kept saying it, over and over and over. 'No, no, no, no.' Never saying it with any more feeling, like he was angry, just a flat no. Sweat still ran down his round cheeks, picking its way between his stubble.

The doors of the train opened, up and down the platform. She guessed they were all the same, but she didn't know because they always sat on the seventh bench. Maybe some were opening on the other side, but then that didn't make much sense; this side was the platform.

The door juddered closed. Martin kept up his mantra the whole time, even when his mutterings were lost in the noise of the departing train. Chloe watched it go, until she felt Martin lift his bulk from the bench. She hopped off, the rucksack once again heavy on her back. They didn't have to hold hands on the way home.

'Thursday already, is it? Two chips, curry sauce in the corner,' Val said, soon as he saw them come in.

Martin shuffled up to the counter and made a great show of looking in the glass. 'How many sausages you got today, Val?' He was already grinning.

'Oh, I don't know, four is it?' Val opened the cabinet. 'Wait a minute.' He took up a pair of tongs. 'Seems I missed one.'

'Looks like a good 'un,' Martin said, giggling.

'What's this then?' Val banged the glass with his tongs, trying to reach Martin's fat finger. 'This sausage has a life of its own!'

Both men turned to Chloe, laughing at the joke they made every time. She tried her best to join them.

Still chuckling, Val readied two polystyrene trays. 'Three scoops for you, sausage fingers. Three and a bit for the special little lady. Because, you *are* special, ain't you?'

They looked at her.

'Yes,' she said quietly.

'Yes,' Martin said. 'She's special. Three and a bit, special.'

Val squirted the almost brown sauce in the corner of each tray, and then wrapped them up in the special paper.

'I saw something today,' Chloe said.

'What's that then, my sweet?' Val said, pushing the little chip packages across the counter top.

'I saw a newspaper.'

Val eyed Martin. 'That so?'

'Think so. It was at the end of the platform.'

'Well, gone now, isn't it? Best not to worry 'bout it. Here's your dinner, see?'

Martin took the chips and hurried her out of the shop. He was in such a fluster, walking so quickly, that she wondered if he'd forgotten about their dinner. By the time they normally reached the playground they'd had half the chips.

'Roundabout,' Martin grunted.

Chloe preferred to sit on the swings, but Martin couldn't fit – even in the big kids' swing. She sat down carefully on the opposite side from him, where she could nearly ignore the bitter tang of his sweat as she ate.

'No spinning,' she said.

'No spinning,' he agreed.

They ate in silence, the dim street lights doing a worse job than the moon in lighting up the playground. The see-saw was broken. The climbing frame had been cut away, hack-saw, Martin had said, though Chloe didn't know what that was. Jagged stumps, like thin tree trunks, still rose out of the ground marking where it used to be. Other times she liked to trace lines between them, imagining how high their twists and turns and tangles might have gone. Tonight, holding her half-eaten chips at arm's length she lined them up with the metal stumps, nibbling them until they were just the right size.

'Couldn't've been a newspaper,' Martin said.

She ate another chip, trying not to use up the curry sauce too quickly.

'They don't make newspapers no more, so couldn't've been a newspaper.'

'Could've been a—'

'Couldn't!' Martin said, hitting the roundabout hard enough to make the whole thing shake.

'Okay.'

They didn't go on the swings. She could see part of Martin wanted her to, wanted to push her: he kept half-turning towards them and then having to stop himself. He kept shaking his head the whole time.

At home, Chloe finally took off her rucksack. But before she could do anything else, she had to unpack everything and put it all in the drawers or on the shelves properly. Two batteries; the big kind that, if they weren't so hard, could be sausages themselves. A torch – that was what the batteries were for, though Chloe had never used it. Her colouring book and colouring pencil. A box that rattled, but she didn't know what was inside. An empty picture frame. And, finally, her raincoat.

Martin watched her, making sure everything was put in its place.

'Can I do some colouring?' she said.

He looked up from where he was taking his shoes off. 'Tonight? Colouring on Thursday?'

'Please?' she said, trying her best not to sound so hungry.

'Not too long.'

She lifted the chair closer to the table, not pulling it along the floor; Martin didn't like it when she did that. Putting the colouring book down she looked for a page she hadn't finished. She went from cover to cover, and then back again, until about two thirds of the way in she found a bit of a page's edge that was blank.

Pencil to her lips, she considered what to put there. A pattern? Some kind of animal? A train? No. She shouldn't put a train there. Not sure *what* to do, she just started colouring. She only had the one pencil and, despite the brightly coloured cover of the book, it was grey.

Martin's grip was too tight, too tight and too sweaty. Chloe couldn't find the energy to struggle against it. The week had been hard: Martin was in a bad mood, sometimes sulky, sometimes angry, and though he didn't hurt her he did break a cup. It was yesterday, or the day before, and he banged his head on the cupboard door. He looked like he didn't understand, the shock very real on his face. Casting around, he just picked up the cup from the side and smashed it. They didn't talk about it.

They sat on the seventh bench. She swung her feet, noticing one of her trainers was starting to get a new hole in the toe, so she could see her sock. It would have to be patched.

The sky was darker that night, and it was starting to get colder. In the cold months she wore her jumper to the platform and they wouldn't eat their chips in the playground, but hurry home instead. She didn't like the cold: it lasted too long.

The train arrived, a black wall that hissed and creaked impatiently. The door opened, and this time small lights tried to mark out the metal steps.

'No, no, no, no,' Martin said under his breath.

The door closed and when the train was gone, Chloe shrugged her rucksack back onto her shoulders. They were walking down the platform when something moved on the tracks. Chloe drifted closer, beyond the broken yellow line until she was right at the edge. There it was, pressed up against the low wall of the platform, like it was hiding.

'What you doing?' Martin said, looming over her.

'There's a hole in my shoe.' She wiggled her toe, still kneeling at the edge.

'Bit of fish?'

'Not for me,' she said, standing.

'Me neither.'

She waited until he'd turned round then put her hand in her pocket to feel it: no bigger than a page in her colouring book, she'd still had to fold the newspaper quickly.

'Thursday already, is it?' Val said with his usual toothless smile. He picked up the tongs, ready to put more scratches in his glass display case, but Martin wasn't playing today. He waited by the till, stepping from one foot to the other.

Val raised an eyebrow at Chloe, then readied their dinner. 'Three scoops, and a little extra for you, special. Ain't no one as special as you, not for miles and miles, you know that?'

They ate the chips on the roundabout, backs to each other, maybe for the last time that year. When she'd eaten half, the rest were getting cold, not that she minded.

At home, Martin watched her empty her rucksack and put it all away.

'No colouring,' he said.

'Okay.'

'Hole.'

'What?'

'*Hole*,' he said, narrowing his eyes. 'Fix it.'

She stared at him for a moment, before remembering. 'Now?'

'Yes, now.'

With a sigh, she took off her shoes and brought the sewing box to the table. Moving the chair, the way he liked, she found the fat needle and thread. He sat in the comfy chair with the small electric heater right next to him. Before long he was snoring loudly. She made sure to finish the sewing before risking touching it; she daren't risk taking it out of her pocket, just touch it.

When she got into bed, she pushed the newspaper, still folded, between her thin mattress and the floor.

'What's this?' Martin shouted.

Chloe was in the tiny bathroom, brushing her teeth. She spat quickly and, mouth still covered in toothpaste, hurried to her room. Martin was shaking and his face was turning red. He pointed at her bed.

'I just found it, that's all,' she said, her voice getting squeaky and high. She started to cry.

'Didn't tell me. Didn't tell me!' Martin grabbed her arm and yanked her to the bed. 'Look!'

She had to wipe away her tears to see.

'Look!' Martin said again, pushing her closer to the pale, worn bedsheet.

He hadn't found the newspaper. Instead, she saw hairs. Fine hairs in two ragged, snaking lines.

'What is it?' she said.

'Yours! You. It's yours.' He gestured wildly at her.

Without thinking, she raised a hand to her head.

'No, don't touch!'

But it was too late. Hair came away in her fingers.

'No, no, no, no,' Martin said. He was wringing his hands, sweat breaking out across his forehead.

'What's happening?' she said.

'Get your pack.'

'But . . . but it's Friday.'

'Get your pack. Come on.' But instead of dragging her over to the shelves, he stepped carefully by, not taking his eyes from her.

'Martin, what's happening?'

'Your pack.'

'I'm scared,' she said.

He packed the rucksack himself, showing her each item so she knew it was in there. He wouldn't talk to her, wouldn't answer her questions. He shook the box she wasn't supposed to open and said, 'Later.' When he was busy at the shelves, she stuffed the newspaper into her pocket.

✦✦✦

The platform was empty as usual. Chloe was bored and hungry. They had come straight from home, not stopping at the playground or at the chip shop, which Martin said was closed. 'But it's *Friday*,' she kept saying. He wouldn't listen, just carried on towards the train station. He didn't even hold her hand.

They sat on the seventh bench all day. She complained but he didn't listen. Eventually, sometime in the afternoon, she was so hungry she started to walk down the platform on her own. He chased after her and, from deep within his coat, found an old chocolate bar, all bent out of shape and the wrapper faded. She ate the whole

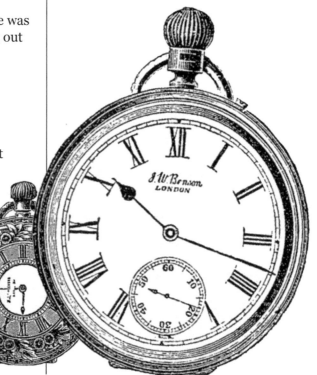

thing in three mouthfuls.

When it started to get dark, she began to feel scared again.

'Martin, it's Friday. Train doesn't come on Friday.'

'Does.'

'We come on Thursday. Thursday, not Friday.'

'Does. Train comes every day,' he said, not looking at her.

She was about to reply, when she saw the light at the end of the track. The bell rang out, louder than ever before.

'Let's go, Martin, I don't like it.'

But he had already started saying no.

'I want to go, Martin.' She went to get up, but he stopped her with a heavy hand. 'Martin?'

'No, no, no, no,' he said, until it was lost in the thunder of the train, though his lips kept moving even then.

The door opened and Chloe flinched, not sure who she expected to be standing there. But the steps were empty.

Martin lifted her up and put her on the train. She was too stunned to do anything about it, his strong hands not giving her much of a choice anyway. She thought he'd been sweating as usual, but really he was crying.

'Martin?'

He held her there until the door started to shut.

'Aren't you coming?' she said.

'No.'

And then he was gone, the train moving, and she was alone. She cried, just standing there, until she couldn't cry anymore. She looked down at her hairless arms and gently felt what little was left on her head.

Eventually, she climbed the steps not knowing where else to go or what else to do. They took her to a long, empty carriage without windows. At each table there was a lamp overhead and she sat at the nearest one. She put down her rucksack and took the newspaper from her pocket and spread it on the table.

She couldn't read, not really. She knew her letters but the words were hard. Next to the newspaper she lined up her colouring book. She opened the box that rattled. Inside were four pencils: red, yellow, green, and blue. Martin had saved them for her, for now.

With the red pencil she started to spell out the first big word on the newspaper that she didn't understand. It must have been important, as it was the only one so big and it was all alone.

QUARANTINE

CONTRIBUTORS

★ ★ ★

BARRY CHARMAN is a writer living in North London, England. He has been published in various magazines, including *Ambit, Griffith Review, Aurealis, Popshot Quarterly, The Literary Hatchet* and *The Linnet's Wings.* Barry's short story 'Doom Warnings' appeared in *The Ghastling's* Book Twelve. *www.barrycharman. blogspot.co.uk*

PAMELA KOEHNE-DRUBE is a writer and editor based in west Wales, where the rugged beauty of the Pembrokeshire coast inspires her every day. As a former museum curator and professional historian, she has travelled the world visiting museums and collections most people have never heard of, and that love of the forgotten is what fuels her creativity. Pamela has ghostwritten for both fiction and non-fiction writers all over the world. When she's not writing for other people, she spends her time working on her first full-length novel, which will explore the Arthurian mythology of Wales.

ZUZANNA KWIECIEN is an illustrator and designer. With her practice, she aims to develop bodies of work that capture the visual narrative of the subject and combine it with a distinct atmosphere. As an artist, she values time and effort put into the construction of a high-quality work of art. Find her on Instagram at *@firstaidkiddo. www.behance.net/zuzannakwiecien*

LAURA LEE LUCAS (she/her) is a VONA/ Voices fellow and a member of the Horror Writers Association. Her fiction has appeared in *Graffiti, Bards and Sages Quarterly, Supernatural Tales, Rigorous, Beat the Dust, Falling Star,* and the *Two Hour Transport Anthology 2019.*

ELIN OLAUSSON is a fan of the weird and the unsettling. She has had stories featured in *Luna Station Quarterly, Nightscript,* and anthologies such as *Unburied: A Collection of Queer Dark Fiction* and *Night Terrors Vol. 4.* Her debut short story collection will be published in 2022. Elin's rural childhood made her love and fear the woods, and she firmly believes that a cat is your best companion in life. She lives in Sweden. *www.elinolausson.com*

STEVEN SHEIL is a writer and filmmaker from Nottingham, England. His work has previously been published in *Black Static* and *The Ghastling,* online at *Fudoki, Horla, Horrified* and *Pyre,* and as part of the Black Library anthologies *Invocations, The Harrowed Paths* and *The Accursed.* He is also the writer and director of the feature film *Mum & Dad* (2008). Steven's short story 'Case' appeared in *The Ghastling's* Book Eleven.

DAVID TOWSEY is a lecturer in Creative Writing at the University of South Wales. His first novel, *Your Brother's Blood,* was published in September 2013 by Jo Fletcher Books. Daid co-writes with the author Katherine Stansfield, under the name D.K. Fields. Their first novel, *Widow's Welcome*, was published in August 2019. The rest of the *Tales of Fenest* trilogy followed in 2020 and 2021. He is also one half of the indie games company, Pill Bug Interactive, who have released three titles across PC and Nintendo Switch™.

ASTRID VALLET collects jars and doesn't know what to put in them, cuts her hair herself and only regrets it a little. Their work is featured in *Sonder Magazine*, *The Shoutflower*, *Hecate Magazine*, and *Crow & Cross Keys*, among others. Find them online @astriddoeswrite.

MAUD WOOLF is Scottish writer with a particular interest in speculative fiction. Currently living and writing in Glasgow, her work has been published by a variety of online magazines including *Bandit Fiction, Horla* and *Metaphorosis*. She is represented by the North Lit Agency.

CLAIRE L. SMITH is an Australian author, visual artist and designer. Her artwork draws from themes of the occult, the macabre and the morbidly beautiful while appearing in the pages of The Ghastling Press, Tenebrous Press, Off Limits Press, Ghost Orchid Press and more.

Her debut gothic horror novella, *Helena*, was released from CLASH Books in 2020, with her next horror novella *When We Entered That House* arriving from Off Limits Press in October 2021. *www.clairelsmith.com*

ANDREW ROBINSON is a printmaker and graphic designer. A self-taught artist specialising in linocut prints, his interests and influences stem from wildlife, mythology, and all things creepy or otherworldly. Andrew hails from the east coast of Canada and now lives in Oxford, England, with his partner and daughters. A selection of his work can be seen at *monografik.ca* and on Instagram @eaglesnakefight.

REBECCA PARFITT has worked in publishing for over a decade. Her debut poetry collection, *The Days After*, was published by Listen Softly London in 2017. She is currently working on a book of macabre short stories for which she won a Writers' Bursary from Literature Wales in 2020. Two stories from this collection were published in *The New Gothic Review* in 2020. Her first film, *Feeding Grief to Animals*, was commissioned in 2020 by the BBC & FfilmCymruWales. She lives in the Llynfi Valley, Wales, with her partner and children. *rebeccaparfitt.com*

DEMON BARBER
RAZORS
ALWAYS READY FOR USE

Manufactured of the **BEST QUALITY** of Refined and Highly Tempered **ENGLISH STEEL.** By a Special Process of Tempering & Hardening, each blade attains an exactness and Equability of Temper with which no English - Ground Razor can compete.

The Flexibility of the Blade makes Shaving a Luxury, even to those with Stubborn Beards and Tender Skin. They **NEVER REQUIRE GRINDING**, and if Stropped with care before and after use on a strop made specially for use with German-Ground Razors, **WILL LAST FOR YEARS.**

RHYS OWAIN WILLIAMS is a writer and editor from Swansea, Wales. His first poetry collection, *That Lone Ship*, was published by Parthian in 2018. Rhys also runs *The Crunch* – a multimedia poetry magazine (*crunchpoetry. com*). In addition to all things ghastly, Rhys is interested in folklore, urban myth and psychogeography. He lives in a terraced house near the sea with his partner and a black cat named Poe. *rhysowainwilliams.com*

WALLACE MCBRIDE is a graphic designer from South Carolina, USA. His work has been featured in *Fangoria*, The Sleepy Hollow International Film Festival, The Boston Comedy Festival, the Associated Press, the U.S. Army and dozens of newspapers in the United States, and also used on official merchandise for *The Prisoner* and *Star Trek*. He is the creator of The Collinsport Historical Society, a website dedicated to the cult television series *Dark Shadows*. Since its launch in 2012, The Collinsport Historical Society has been recognised numerous times by The Rondo Hatton Classic Horror Awards, and received The Silver Bolo Award in 2020 from Shudder's *The Last Drive-In with Joe Bob Briggs*. Wallace sometimes uses the handle 'Unlovely Frankenstein', which is either a pseudonym or just the name of his Etsy store. He isn't sure yet. *www.unlovelyfrankenstein.com*

APRIL-JANE ROWAN is an author, editing assistant for Gurt Dog Press and social media co-ordinator for both Gurt Dog Press and *The Ghastling*. She was born with a morbid fascination that she turned into writing so she could explain away her strangeness. Luckily for her, she found she rather liked it, so for many years she has been creating bizarre, dark tales. Her books *Beneath A Bethel* and *Lovelorn* are available from Gurt Dog Press. When not writing, she can be found lurking in graveyards, libraries and museums. She lives in Sweden with her two partners and their pack of beasties. Follow her on Instagram at @theliterarychamber

It's Amazing!

The low cost of supporting
The Ghastling!

*For just pennies a day you can support
the morbid interests of horror fans all over the world*

VISIT **WWW.PATREON.COM/THEGHASTLING**
TO FIND OUT HOW YOU CAN BECOME A GHASTLING

Lightning Source UK Ltd.
Milton Keynes UK
UKHW050310230722
406241UK00003B/86

9 781838 189143